ANONYMOUS

A NOVEL

W9-DDD-327

JASON TANAMOR

ISBN-10: 1434838285
ISBN-13: 978-1434838285

This book was printed in the United States.

Also by Jason Tanamor:

Hello Lesbian!
The Extraordinary Life of Shady Gray

Praise for *Anonymous*:

"*Anonymous* is one of those margin hugging novels that toes the line between a dark, edgy, cult gem and a commercial bestseller, and should satisfy aficionados of both." - Book Knurd

"...there are moments of great humor and swaths of excellent storytelling that make the book a fun read..." - Mark J. Lehman, Amazon Reviews

"...reveling in the vagaries of unreliable narration, Tanamor proves himself a master of the existential mystery: the question is never whodunit, but who is the 'who,' and how do we know that the 'it' ever really got done?" – Small Press Reviews

"A good fun read, short and sweet; these characters and their stories will stay with you!" - Brett Starr, Amazon Reviews

"*Anonymous* is a nice surprise, worth reading for those into slightly experimental fiction..." - Richard Stoehr, Amazon Reviews

"Reading *Anonymous* is like taking an audio tour of a high security jail, the tales told will shock, challenge and amuse in equal measure. Tanamor has a gift for skimming the scum from the top of a boiling pot of rancid emotion and making you taste it.." – Matt Adcock, Dark Matters Reviews

1.

Stories are what make the world go round. Stories, they entice people. They influence. They engage. There are stories of emotion. Pick up the paper and you'll see a group of miners trapped for weeks. The miners, they use each other for support until they're rescued. One by one by one, each miner is pulled out, his body scratched and bruised but the expression on his face, it's why people are so hopeful. There is relief from the community and the miners, they're grateful for all the assistance.

There are stories of happiness. A mother and daughter reunited after 30 years when they were separated by adoption. The mother, who was just a teenager when she gave birth, it was the best and worst decision she'd ever made. It wasn't until a chance encounter at a grocery store that the reunion was made possible. Now, the two are best friends and have lunch together weekly.

And then there are stories for those who watch the news about some tragic event, and now they're being asked to give money to help the grieving family.

The child, he's bald and pasty white, sickly thin, standing behind his mother while she pleads to the country. He looks sick, but in reality, it's his mother who is sick. He holds a teddy bear close to his body for effect. It makes people watching go, "Awe, poor thing."

Hundreds, thousands of dollars, loads of money are being forwarded to a P.O. Box somewhere in Nebraska, and later, victims are finding out that the story is bogus. The story, it's filled with too many uncertainties, too many holes.

People are finding out that there isn't an ill child, and that in reality there's a crazy mother who shaved her child's head and spoon fed him cold medicine until he looked like he had undergone a series of medical procedures.

A sympathetic cry out on television, 24-hour news channels, and people, viewers, innocent victims, after the truth is revealed, they're saying to themselves, "That's the last time I do something good. That's the last time I trust people." These people are saying to themselves, "Fuck people!" These people will never donate money toward a cause again.

Now, they're looking at every person with suspicion, wondering what exactly the person wants from them. A scruffy looking man standing on the corner of the highway with a sign that reads, "DISABLED VET. PLEASE HELP," he's being questioned by people driving by. His coat is ripped and faded from the sun, and his pants have holes in the knees. His fingernails, they're dirt black from being without water and his lone backpack, it's dusty and muddy from debris that gets kicked up.

"Why don't these people get jobs?" they say, as they pass by in their cars.

They say, "Go down to McDonald's and work the register." They say this about the scruffy looking man, all because they were conned by an honest looking mother on television. Everybody to them is a question mark. Forget about all the heartfelt stories of good, hope and miracle. There's a saying that says, "One bad apple spoils the bunch." This mother, she's one bad apple. She's now serving time for fraud and child endangerment.

Her spoon fed child, his head is now full of hair, and he has his entire life in front of him. He's now free to live a normal life, well, normal in the respect that each month his mother used to starve him, shave his head and hide cold medicine in his grape juice.

Things like that don't tend to come up in conversation. "My family used to go to Disneyland every summer. What about you?"

And this child, trying to cope with his life, now parent free, he says, "I had the typical childhood. You know, your mother feeds you Sudafed and makes you look sickly all so she can con money from people like your parents. The normal stuff."

The victims, these innocent people, were conned by an anonymous person, someone they didn't know, someone who showed up at the right time and at the right place, and being a victim, that's all you can say about this experience.

The anonymous are the ones that influence society, they are the ones that steer culture, they are the ones that get laws changed, and they are the ones that get laws enacted. The anonymous are ones that you peg down for being soccer moms, when in reality they are running a grow house and shipping plants of marijuana weekly from their basements. Plants that eventually get hauled out by police officials, their value is close to half a million dollars.

The child, tablespoon fed with Sudafed was often neglected by his mother. This type of love only disengages a person from his surroundings. Who else's household has dozens of four ounce bottles of cough and cold medicine filled to the ceiling in the bathroom cabinet? According to his mother, in her statement given to the judge, it was the most profitable $11.59 per bottle investment she'd ever made.

In court, she's showing remorse for her actions, all while standing handcuffed in an oversized orange jumpsuit. Her cheeks are red from crying and her nose, it's wet from sniffling. She stutters when she talks and her voice, it's quiet and shaky.

Photos of her child displayed on easels like they are artwork convince the jury that you just don't know about people based on their looks. One juror, she says, "She looks like my mother. How could she do this to her child? I guess you never know about people until you get to know them."

You can't spot them as easily as toupees. It's you, the victim, who gives them the benefit of the doubt. People aren't stupid. They just want to believe in others. They just want to believe that the world isn't coming to an end. And more importantly, they just want to believe in themselves. They want to believe that they can still trust their fellow human being to do the right thing.

"Back in the day," people will tell you, "we never locked our door. Not for 30 years we didn't. Back then, you could walk next door and borrow a cup of sugar. Nowadays, you don't even look at people for fear of them thinking you're giving them a dirty look."

Today, people don't even know their neighbor's name, much less what she looks like. Every now and then, they'll see her walking out of her house with sunglasses on and her hair pulled back in a ponytail.

People don't think twice about their neighbor, only that she keeps to herself and that her child doesn't have any friends. It is not until the newspapers highlight their story that gossip begins to spread. It is not until the mother is convicted that gossip begins to take over dinner conversations. And it is not until the mother is sentenced to a mental health facility that gossip begins to relate to each neighbor on the block. People, they're saying, "Maybe it's time we get to know our neighbors." They're saying, "Maybe it's time to dust off that China and have a dinner party."

According to Unknown, an anonymous and proud of it, "This is how we matter to society." He says, "Without us, there wouldn't be an Amber Alert. Without us, there wouldn't be a Neighborhood Watch Program." He says this as if it's normal to act this way. People, they're saying, "Without anonymous, there wouldn't be mental health institutions."

According to the dictionary, anonymous lack individuality and distinction. They have no distinctive character or recognition factor. Anytime you see an anonymous photo, it usually is of a silhouette man, about yay high and yay weight. Have you seen this person?

Currently, Unknown is in prison for posing as a celebrity's manager. Now, the conned restaurants and hotels, they're being extra cautious whenever future Unknown's call. Like the disabled veteran on the side of the highway, managers are questioning each person that walks through the door.

"Society needs low-life's, they better the world," Unknown says. "Without them, there wouldn't be improvements." He says this as he believes it. He says this because he's a low-life. He says this because he's disconnected from the world.

Unknown is in prison for deception, he's in prison for fraud, and he's in prison for trademark infringement. He says, "I was using Tom Cruise's name, Brad Pitt's name, and Colin Farrell's name. I was using them to my advantage."

Without Unknown, restaurants and hotel chains wouldn't have added procedures to prevent these cons from happening. And this is the thanks he gets - a prison sentence.

This is Unknown. One of the many anonymous low-life's that society "deals with." If you ask someone who has been conned by Unknown what happened and by whom, the answer inevitably would be, "I don't know. Someone. A no name. He was anonymous."

The conned are extra cautious now and anytime they see a family on the news crying out to help find their lost child they're thinking, "What else is on television?"

These are those types of stories.

2.

Seriously, he wants to be in the "in" crowd.

He tells people that he's friends with this celeb, that celeb, high profile celebrities that wouldn't give him the time or day.

He says to anyone that will listen, "Tom Cruise? I'm his manager." Then he drinks his martini and orders another round for the group of patrons he's somehow managed to con into listening to him. These patrons are usually women, beautiful women, long legged women with perfect breasts and perfect hair. Women that will do anything to meet a big star.

These women, women he has no chance with, are the ones he's into. These women are the type that read the entertainment magazines and buy into the latest fad diets and workout routines hoping that one day, their bodies can look like Angelina Jolie's or Scarlett Johansson's. "Apply makeup like the stars?" These women are eating up the articles and spending hundreds on products. "Reese Witherspoon's children only eat yellow foods?" Now, these women's children only eat yellow foods.

Three women stare at him as he downs the drink with no care whatsoever of the tab amount. It's reaching $700 dollars. But he's not counting, because if you ask him, he's Tom Cruise's manager and, well let's just go from there.

The three women - the lipstick woman, the buxom woman, and legs - they all look at each other. They're impressed at this frivolous man that has presented a much better evening than they had planned. Of course, planning to meet Tom Cruise is never on the agenda. Unless you're a stalker. And even then, meeting Tom Cruise takes scheming; it's never as easy as this.

When you're hiding out in bushes to meet your favorite celebrity, well, that's just pathetic. When you're designing an elaborate plan to get laid, that's just creepy.

"He's doing press right now," Unknown says, "he'll call me when he's done." He looks at his watch to give the impression that Tom Cruise is running late. Tom Cruise is always late. In fact, he's still late, from the last time he didn't show and the time before that.

The man, Unknown, he does this anytime he's feeling irrelevant. At expensive restaurants, fancy clubs, wherever there are people of influence. He does this wherever there is culture to be steered.

Such as the case here, at this establishment downtown. The man, known only as Unknown, whips out his phone and dials a number. It's the same number he uses every time. The lettering on the phone's number pad is faded so you can't tell if the digit is a three or an eight.

Leaking out of the receiver, ringing is heard, and then voice mail.

He says into his phone, "Cruise, it's Unknown. Where are you?" Then he flips down the lid and sticks the phone back into his jacket pocket. Somewhere a few miles away, Unknown's home answering machine is filled with messages similar to this.

"Seriously, you're like an hour late," and "What the fuck dude?" are his favorites. He says these lines while eyeing each woman. Secretly, as he's talking, he's undressing each lady and envisioning what they look like naked.

One of the girls sitting next to him, she turns to her friend and smiles seductively. She thinks she's going to meet Tom Cruise. "So, he's really coming?" she says, primping her hair with her newly manicured fingers.

Her lips, they've been glossed and re-glossed with several brushes of lipstick. Next to her, there are napkins with lips impressions, some smudged and some fresher than others. The corner of the table looks like an origami project gone horribly wrong.

Unknown smiles. His body, it's leaning back on the nice cushion at the round table off to the side. The table is the VIP table. It's away from the rest of the seats, making everyone in the restaurant know that it's for important people only.

Occasionally, random diners, they look toward Unknown, their thoughts of who and why. A famous writer, a businessman people think. Perhaps an attorney. Women always think it's money. This person must have money.

A woman across the room stares at Unknown and then to the women. She shakes her head in disgust and wonders the worst of this situation. Then, she returns back to her plate of spaghetti that's on special for $9.99, stuffing her face with her fork. Oh, and you get free garlic sticks tonight with every entrée. She's just happy to be out for the night. No cooking, dirty dishes, nothing. Had she been 50 pounds lighter and 10 years younger, she could have been sitting at the table waiting for Tom Cruise to appear.

"Got his voice mail," Unknown says, as he sits back into the cushion. The thickness, it forces Unknown's body to go back a few inches. The seat's cushion, it now has a perfect indentation of Unknown's back.

Unknown, he's a celebutante, a term he made up while sitting on his raggy recliner eating chips from the bag. A far cry from the booth he's enjoying right now. His recliner is partly made of duct tape, spread evenly down the sides and across the chair's arms. They look like racing stripes and as a joke, Unknown pretends that his recliner is a race car going 200 miles per hour. At times, he watches NASCAR and pretends that he's in the driver's seat.

Unknown, he's a wannabe socialite whose real life sees appointments, post office runs, and grocery store drop-ins. His life sees ATM stops and movie rental returns. In the microwave is the stench of burnt popcorn. The knob is missing on the stove's burner control. Often, he has to turn it with a wrench just to make it burn. This is Unknown's real life.

His apartment, it pales in comparison to the lifestyle he suggests he lives. The wallpaper is peeling in certain areas, while water spots hang above him on the ceiling. The carpet, it's faded from years and years of shampooing and vacuuming, and Unknown's wondering if he should buy more. The walls, they're very thin and at times, he can hear his neighbors yelling. F-this, F-that, then a lamp against the plaster. "At some point," he says, "that wall will have a hole the size of a lamp." Every now and then, there's humping up above him. The lady who lives above Unknown, she's a rabbit. Squeak-a, squeak-a, squeak-a. In different rhythms, and at different times of the day. The picture frames on his wall are never in the same position. One day they're tilted right, the next they're tilted left. The positions depend on how hard the upstairs neighbor is getting it from behind. Have you ever seen picture frames Salsa dance? Go to Unknown's apartment.

Unknown's days go by with no excitement; there's nothing to fill his inner desire. He doesn't have a job anymore because disability pays his monthly rent and bills.

Apparently, being mentally ill is a cause to not work. In Unknown's case, mental illness is only half of his problem. Sex addiction is the other half with bad furniture coming in a distant third. Oh, and the sound of stomping above interjected with "huh, huh, huh" noises? That comes in a close fourth.

However, at night, this is what Unknown does. He cons people by using big name celebrities, saying that he's their manager. Other clients Unknown says he has are Colin Farrell, Brad Pitt and Christian Bale. He says this to the restaurant manager, the club owner, whoever is the boss, whoever will listen.

Unknown says, "They're filming a movie here." And when that happens, you can bet the manager, the club owner, whoever will never check the papers to see if city blocks are closed down for filming.

Sometimes there's a notice, sometimes there's not. It's usually a single box, no bigger than two inches by two inches, hidden in between a personal ad featuring a DWF and an ad selling an old console television. "Antique. Good condition. $200.00. Or best offer."

"Is he your only client?" one woman says, anxious to know more, as she applies another coat of lipstick. Her lips are full, moist from her drink. Her lips, they now extend a quarter inch from her face. It's like a third coat of paint to hide an imperfection. Gradually, the shade gets darker and darker until it begins to peel.

Unknown name drops Pitt, Bale and Colin Farrell. One time he mentioned Zac Efron but the young, hip actor was so famous in the teenage girl category that most of Unknown's victims had no idea who he was referring to. If he were into little girls, well, that would be his fifth problem.

The con man, Unknown, he says, "I tell Colin to watch his language all the time." Then he shakes his head and holds up his empty glass to the waiter.

"Another round," he says. "Just put it on my tab."

His tabs are complimentary. They're always complimentary. What he does is call ahead of time introducing himself as so-and-so's manager. He says, "I'll be coming in with Tom Cruise later today. Get a table ready for us." He adds that he expects his bill to be complimentary.

The restaurant manager, knowing that this is a huge honor to have such a big star in his establishment says, "Of course, of course." The restaurant never checks references, living by the motto that the customer is always right. Or maybe the manager just wants to believe that people are genuinely honest in life. Or maybe the manager has not stumbled upon a down on her luck mother pleading for money to help her sick child.

Then Unknown shows up, alone, saying that Cruise, or Pitt, or Farrell is running late. He's doing press and that he'll get here as soon as possible. "Press junkets," he says. "Tom's a busy man, but he'll be here as soon as possible."

Blocks away is Unknown's beat up and rusted out car parked in between an expensive BMW and Mercedes Benz. The bumper is falling of and he's had this car for a decade. The dash where the stereo goes is empty from the time his unit was stolen in a string of burglaries on his block. The glove compartment is tied to the latch so that it doesn't fall open. To Unknown, this isn't a big deal as the only thing in his glove compartment is a broken air conditioner knob from his dash panel.

The car was a gift from his godparents, who urged him to get out and meet people when they realized he hadn't left the house for months. Unknown was a 20-something-year-old virgin with no job, no education and no social skills. His mother was a lowlife as well; it's probably where Unknown got it.

At first, Unknown's godparents thought they were coddling him, or in their words, "protecting" him from the anonymous people out there ready to take advantage. After all, he was without a mother and who really knows what happened when he was under her control?

When they first took Unknown in, he was shy and introverted. Years of abuse does this to a child. So, the decision to "care" for him became a priority.

Whenever he bounced a check, his godmother would call the bank for him. Whenever he had a complaint, his godmother would talk to the manager. And whenever Unknown was feeling lonely, his godmother bought him a nice television with premium cable. To anyone that would ask, she'd say, "We just need to make sure that he doesn't have any side effects. Let's just let him be for a while. Let him get accustomed to his home."

With abuse, a child is forced to imagine a better life. With loneliness, a child is forced to imagine a better life. It's a coping mechanism when your real life offers very little.

Now? Unknown's godparents are proud of him for getting out into the real world. Amongst the thousands of messages to himself there are phone calls from his godparents telling him that they love him, and that they are proud of him, and that if he needs anything to not hesitate and call. To them, they did a fine job in raising their godchild.

Unknown says to the waiter, "He'll be here shortly. While I wait, I'll start off with an appetizer and some drinks." The waiter disappears only to return with several entrees and drinks, all of which are complimentary. All of which are in the higher priced section of the menu.

As he's sitting there sipping on expensive martinis and indulging himself with $30 dollar food dishes, word gets around that Tom Cruise will be arriving and that the guy sitting over there is his manager. An anonymous phone call to the hostess from an obsessed fan leaks word that he saw on E! that Tom Cruise's new movie is being filmed.

The hostess, a high-school student working part-time, smiles from ear to ear and joins in on the excitement. "I love the 'Mission Impossible' movies," she says into the phone. Not once does she question the caller.

Unknown's cell phone is like the Yellow Pages. Every restaurant and night club's phone number in the city is saved.

Unknown, he invites a table of beautiful women over to join him and runs up high tabs, which go unpaid courtesy of the legend of Tom Cruise.

Or the legend of Brad Pitt.

Or the legend of Colin Farrell. Colin Farrell, he swears all the time and Unknown, well, he's trying to get him to ease off on the curse words.

Unknown whips out his phone again, from his cashmere top coat, his favorite outfit, and pushes redial. "Cruise, where are you?" The phone machine at his apartment, it flickers its bright red digits, adding another call to the list. Unknown, he flips down the lid to his phone and slides it into his inner pocket.

An hour goes by, the table covered with empty glasses, the glasses with smeared lipstick on the edges, and stacked plates that have all gone eaten by, not only Unknown, but the three women as well, and the manager comes out asking if everything is fine.

Unknown says, "I'm sorry, Tom is extremely busy and it looks like he won't be making it after all." His body is calm from the alcohol and his attitude is a winning one. His alcoholic haze has him seeing six women, three sets of twins.

The manager, disappointed with the news, smiles in defeat and says, "Of course, of course. Maybe next time." Then he, along with the waiter, removes the plates and glasses. He says, "I still pick up your tab." He says this hoping for another time. He says this because he believes in people.

On the entertainment programs, witnesses come forward to say that their favorite celebrity always eats at such and such place and orders the same thing each time. Like clockwork, you can always catch a glimpse of your favorite actor. A show like this sticks in your head if you're plopped in front of the TV long enough. And if your godmother coddles you your entire post-abuse life, at some point your brain develops in a way that is unhealthy.

Unknown smiles, his bill reaching $1000 dollars, and says, "I promise you." Then he looks at the three women, each with her own agenda, and says, "Maybe next time girls."

Unknown says, "Anyone interested in a night cap?" This anonymous man, he's very blunt. His quote unquote star power and complimentary meals give him the leverage he needs to take one or two or all three of these women back to his hotel room. A room that's also complimentary by using the same tactic.

He says to the hotel manager, "Tom's staying at a nearby hotel under an assumed name." He jokes, saying the name is George Clooney. "Not really, but you get the drift," he says.

And if they're lucky, he might even stop in and say hi to them. He might even sign some autographs and take some photos. He says, "Wouldn't that be great?"

Like the restaurant manager, the hotel supervisor comps his room, a suite, hoping for the chance to meet Tom Cruise. Like the witnesses on television, the supervisor wants to say that Tom Cruise stayed at his wonderful hotel and tipped very well. Unknown, he knows the power of celebrity.

One woman agrees and she and Unknown vanish from the restaurant. They walk into the hotel lobby, waving to the night staff. "Have a good night, folks," they say. Unknown, he escorts his guest to the penthouse suite and the two take advantage of the amenities that the hotel offers.

After a soak in the hot tub, utilizing the mini-bar and ordering from room service, Unknown takes advantage of his guest, wearing off the several coats of lipstick from her face.

Unknown does this anytime he feels irrelevant. The same routine beginning with a couple phone calls. His answering machine, filled with messages from himself that say nothing more than, "where are you?" blinks its red indicator light, showing how many new messages he has. One message lost in the batch says, "Hi honey, your father and I want you to come over this Saturday for pizza and movies. Any suggestions on a movie?"

"Hi, I'd like to speak to the manager," Unknown says, to the disembodied voice that answers. He says, "I'm Brad Pitt's manager and he's in town doing some promotional work for an upcoming movie he's starring in with Tom Cruise."

The lies, they just roll off his tongue like that. He's done it so many times, he's an expert. He's done it so many times, he believes them himself.

Through the receiver, Unknown can hear a young woman's voice get higher, excited by the fact that her Pitt will be in town. He waits until the enthusiasm dies down, knowing that his scam will work like a charm.

Unknown says, "We'd like to come in for dinner but are in a hurry so if you could get a table ready for us, that would be great." Above him, the neighbor is experimenting with tantric positions from the Middle East. He looks up at his ceiling, drywall falling down onto his floor, and hears the groans escape his neighbor as she moves from corner to corner.

"Of course, of course," the manager says, her voice holding back the excitement. Before Unknown can ask for courtesy, she says, "It's on the house."

"And please," Unknown says, "keep this on the down low." He says this, but deep down he loves the attention. "Women can't keep secrets," he says. The near sighting will spread in no time.

The newspaper, there's a two inch by two inch notice saying that blocks will be closed for filming. And then detours down other streets. From this date to this date, and we're sorry for the inconvenience.

Unknown hangs up the phone and waits, for show time. The lady upstairs, her vagina must be the size of a double wide by now. Next door, Unknown is surprised there is still furniture left to be thrown. He says this as he straightens the picture frames just because. He says this as he waits for his phone call to make its rounds through the establishment.

Fifteen minutes before he's supposed to arrive, he makes a quick phone call to the restaurant saying that Pitt is running late and if it would be alright if he came in and had a few drinks.

The restaurant manager, she says, "Of course, of course. We'll have a table ready for you." Then she hangs up and rushes to clear a corner table with dim lighting. And Unknown, he heads out for the night, leaving the neighbors to fight and fuck, both at the same time.

Parked in his car blocks away, Unknown pulls down the driver side visor to check himself in the mirror. The edges of the visor are frayed and one corner is taped together. In the back seat are stacks of entertainment and men's health magazines.

A large suitcase is in the trunk filled with various outfits for the occasion. There's a retro leather jacket to go along with his faded jeans with holes in the knees. A couple vintage button down long sleeve shirts are folded neatly on top of each other. Different pairs of shoes he's accumulated for each outfit, they are spread out evenly across the bottom of the suitcase. Stashed along the side of the clothes is a box of condoms. Various types of condoms that include ribbed, sensitive, flavored and self-lubricated. Like the restaurants and hotels are accommodating to Unknown is the same way he is accommodating to women.

The manager, her suit ironed and makeup plastered on her face, a feeling of elation inside, says to her staff, "He'll be here in ten." Her hair is pinned back tightly on her head, a single strand falling down the side of her face. She's done her best to avoid steam or liquids that would force her to lock herself in the restroom to redo it.

Unknown enters with confidence, his body with grandiose posture and his head up, his aura engaging those around him. The manager and her staff, they are lined up with perfect posture and bright faces. He says, "I expect him here in a few."

A group of waitresses has timed it perfectly to be in between tables and refills, with a few girls holding pitchers of water and iced tea. One waitress has a dish of meatloaf that has gotten cold courtesy of the legend of Brad Pitt. To the diner, however, the meatloaf can be nuked and she apologizes for the inconvenience. Brad Pitt is definitely worth the extra dollar lost in tip.

In front of the patrons, Unknown is led by the manager to a lone table off in the corner. The waitresses stand and watch until the two are no longer seen. Then they return to their respective tables with excuses already made up. "There was a mix up in the kitchen," or "I'm sorry, we had to change out the iced tea."

A single light hangs above and a candle burns in the center of the lone VIP table. A folded piece of cardboard reads RESERVED FOR MR. PITT in sharp calligraphy.

The manager says, "Anything you want. It's on the house." She smiles and walks away, only to hide behind the counter in the kitchen, where she stares at Unknown, as he breezes through the menu. She says to herself, "My Pitt is coming in. To my restaurant." She bites down on her bottom lip and obsesses.

Unknown orders his usual five entrees and mixed drinks, his tab once again reaching a limit his credit card couldn't handle. And like before, word somehow slips through that Brad Pitt is coming, Brad Pitt is coming.

Women, shameless women, some with dates and some married, they make excuses and then shimmy past Unknown and smile sensually. They go to the restroom to freshen up, they say they have to make a phone call, or that something needs adjusting, always making it a point to pass by Unknown's table, even though the pathway is nowhere near their own.

Unknown says, "Hello. Would you like to join me?" He pulls out the chair to his right and, while a few women decline, a couple do.

"Unknown," he says. "I'm Brad Pitt's manager." The women, shaking in their heels, extend a hand to Unknown. He kisses the top of each and orders drinks for them. Anything on the top shelf works.

Like clockwork, Unknown reaches in for his phone and flips the cover and dials home. A couple rings go by and the voice mail picks up. The answering machine is in the kitchen, on the counter pushed back to the corner. Next to it is a case of pop that just reads COLA on it. Unknown's real top shelf consists of generic, on sale, marked down for expiration date and two for one.

The voice mail says, "This is Brad, leave a message." Unknown turns the volume up on his phone ahead of time so that the women can hear the announcement through his phone. They turn and address each other, with one woman biting down on her bottom lip to hide a smile, and the other staring with bulging eyes. The two can't believe this is happening.

Unknown says, "Pitt, where are you?" Then he hangs up and flips down the lid and replaces the cell back in his inner pocket. Around his apartment, the neighbors continue fighting and fucking. On the walls, the picture frames are doing a jig from left to right and back again.

"Actors," he says. He says this jokingly for playful conversation. Although the women giggle, they don't say a word, still nervous and slightly intimidated by this man who knows Brad Pitt.

"You two can relax," he says, smiling to each individually. One woman laughs awkwardly and then drinks from her glass. The other, she still can't believe this is happening. Her eyes, they're locked on Unknown, bulging to a point they might fall out.

More drinks come and plates of hot food arrive. He says to the server, "You're doing a fine job." She takes away empty glasses and reports back to the manager.

The manager, still holding her position behind the counter, checks her watch. It's been an hour and a half. No Pitt. She checks the door and then her watch. Then she regains her position and continues staring.

She calculates the total in her head and begins to get skeptical. After a couple breaths, the manager straightens her shirt and disappears out of the kitchen.

"You have a fine establishment here," Unknown says, the manager now within earshot. She walks up to the table, her body stern and ready for answers.

"I just called, he should be here shortly," Unknown says. He says, "I'm sure he'll love your hospitality." He squints to see the manager's name badge. "Tanya," he says.

The two women, they simultaneously turn to the manager to confirm the phone call, nodding their heads up and down. One woman, her smile is frozen while the other, her mouth is open and her eyes are strained.

The manager's body calms. She says, "Of course. If you need anything, just let me know." In her mind, there's still hope. She escapes into the kitchen and tells the server that her Pitt should be coming anytime now and that the man had just talked to him.

They rejoice like school girls, shaking their hands as they meet in between their bodies and, together, stare from behind the counter.

Unknown says, "Are you ladies big fans?"

One woman, sipping her margarita, sets the glass down and says, "I love his movies." The other woman just sits and nods her head, her eyes still bigger than normal, hoping that she will soon be sitting at the same table as Brad Pitt. Her body, it doesn't move, it is still like a mannequin.

A few awkward moments go by, eerie silences in between drinks, and Unknown reaches for his phone. He pushes redial and, again, after a few rings that leak out from the receiver for the women to hear, the voice mail triggers. "Brad, it's Unknown. Where are you?" He says this with an uncompromising voice, as if he means business.

He says, "I'm sitting here with two lovely ladies. We're having drinks, waiting for you." He pauses and says, "Tell Angelina and the kids I said, 'hi.'" Then he closes his phone again and slides it into his inner breast pocket.

The bill, now above $1200 dollars, sits on the computer as the manager watches it ring up more and more drinks, and more and more food. "How much more food can they eat?" she says. The bill, it's something that she will be explaining to the General Manager at their next meeting.

Twenty minutes have passed since her last visit and she sees that the restaurant is closing in less than an hour. Her Pitt needs to arrive soon.

Unknown, on the brink of drunkenness, downs another martini and says, "I can't believe Brad didn't show." His voice is slurring and his eyes are getting heavy.

He says, "He'll hear about it tomorrow. Trust me." The women, looks of exasperation, look at each other and then to Unknown.

One says, "What now?" She's sloshed herself and feels guilty drinking for free all night. In a roundabout way she feels if she's with Brad Pitt's manager, she'll have a story to tell for life. An "oh yeah?" story, one that plays out like a six degrees of separation. If you sleep with someone, you sleep with every person that person has slept with. Unless of course, it's Brad Pitt's manager, then you've one upped them.

The other woman, her eyes now tired, says, "Do you have a room nearby?"

And Unknown, once again, seeing that his plan is working as usual, says he does, and that it would be a good idea if the three go back and party.

They agree and stand, the manager bolting from the kitchen to see what's going on. She says, "He couldn't make it?" her voice nonchalant and reaching disappointment.

"Maybe next time," Unknown says.

The four stand in a circle by the table when a woman yells out, "He's here! He's here!"

The newspaper, there's a two inch by two inch notice saying that blocks will be closed for filming. And then detours down other streets. From this date to this date, and we're sorry for the inconvenience.

The manager, the two women, and Unknown focus their attention to the front and see Brad Pitt standing there, waiting to be catered to. The hostess, she points over to Unknown's table and Pitt shakes his head, his shoulders shrugging.

"Your manager's over there," she says, pointing to Unknown specifically. Pitt turns toward the door, and a man enters.

"This is my manager." Pitt turns and the man extends his hand out for a shake.

"Please to meet you," he says to the hostess.

The restaurant manager walks quickly up to the front and introduces herself. She tells Pitt what happened and the next thing they know the police is there.

Witnesses give their statements, saying things like, "This guy came in and acted like he was Brad Pitt's manager so he could score free food and chicks." The cops, they divide their officers with some making arrests and others questioning the manager and the two women.

Unknown, his gig is up. His feeling of irrelevancy, it's back. And his godparents, they're leaving messages on his machine asking if he likes action flicks.

The police officials are hauling Unknown out of the restaurant in handcuffs. This is the most exciting thing that has happened all night.

The manager is getting her photo taken with Brad Pitt. The high bill was worth it, even if it didn't go exactly as planned.

Unknown, he's now sitting in prison, a concrete rectangle with a barred up window, reflecting on his life. He does this when he's feeling irrelevant.

And to those he's conned, they're thinking, anonymous did this. There was nothing really special about this man. He was just some man.

3.

Unknown wants the anonymous to feel how he wants to feel, like they're wanted, like they matter. This derealization of what's real in society causes Unknown to separate himself from the outside world.

When he was a kid, he'll tell you, in school, the class decided to put notes in helium balloons, only to let them fly away to wherever. This exercise, done by his teachers in previous classes, it was fun and exciting and gave the students a chance to meet people from other parts of the country.

The teacher, upon releasing the balloons, says, "You never know, the person you meet could influence your life as an adult."

Unknown, his note folded neatly, trapped inside a red balloon for someone out there to find, flies out of his hand, being taken by the wind. He watches it go, and then weeks, many weeks later, a letter in the mail at his mother's house tells him that his note was found. A pen pal relationship develops, and it's not for a year or so Unknown discovers that his "friend" is actually a convicted child molester trying to get down his pants.

This "friend," he's writing to set up a week that he can come down and meet Unknown in person. He says, "I feel like we've got a special bond. I'd like to take that bond to a more personal level." And just like that, Unknown's friend, he's seen on the news being hauled away in handcuffs, arrested for being a pedophile.

It's funny how childhood experiences stay with you. How the convicted child molester made Unknown feel is how he wants everyone to feel - taken. How the abuse from his mother made him fragile and insecure, it's what he posts upon everyone else. And how his godparents coddled him, keeping away society's bad people, it's how he gains your trust. A pen pal that, instead of exchanging letters, exchanges bodily fluids. The helium balloon is Tom Cruise and where it lands is a table of beautiful women.

Unknown says, "The murderer, he's taken a child's life, his own child, because his wife was cheating on him. It was a statement. His wife, banging whoever, took her husband for granted."

The prison where Unknown is sentenced to has a lot of personality. Each inmate, he represents a new breed of attention. Each inmate, he is the result of a result of a result. And each inmate, he's someone Unknown is interested in.

Unknown floats his helium balloon out into the air. His pen pals are picked by pure coincidence - seemingly.

A murderer, known around the prison as Ambiguous, says he wanted his wife to regret him. The job was a success.

Unknown says, "She won't ever forget Ambiguous now. He made himself matter." And every time he's up for parole, the wife shows up and pleads her side of things. She says her husband has no right to be granted parole. She brings a photograph of their child in for impact. The photo is of the child beaming; there are big alphabet blocks in the background that represent learning. There is hope in his eyes that represents life.

Tears, uncontrollable drops fall down her cheek, almost hitting the picture.

She says, "Like my dead child, my husband shall never have the chance to breathe fresh air again." She tells this to the parole board as she holds the picture up high for all to see. She pulls out a teddy bear and blanket from her purse that she still holds onto closely. It's a constant reminder of her once loved child. The blanket still has her child's scent and the teddy bear's ear shows tiny bite marks from when he was teething.

Sniffle, uncontrollable sniffles until the tears build up around her eyes again. She does this every time Ambiguous is in front of the board. She never makes eye contact with him; rather she flaunts the memory of a lost life.

Weep, uncontrollable weeping until she starts the process all over. Photo, then teddy bear, then blanket, and tears, sniffles and weeping interjected. She says to the parole board, "His mother should have had an abortion. Better yet, a coat hanger abortion." To her, he is invisible, anonymous, a societal reject. To her, he should have been aborted, a contraceptive practice to rid the world of turds.

Ambiguous's wife will never forget him. She knows every little detail about her husband's crime. The baby, innocent, has no idea of what to expect in the world. It is a victim of its own existence. The baby is filled with joy for no apparent reason. It trusts whoever is holding it and its undeveloped brain plays simple images of happiness.

What's more important is that society will never forget Ambiguous. Society, it wants to eliminate those that are a threat to it. "But, no matter what," Unknown says, "we'll always be thought of." He says this, sitting alone in his dark, empty excuse for a home.

This is how Ambiguous matters. Ambiguous was caught a few miles away from the crime, standing on top of a bridge, looking down into the water, the same flowing water his baby was recently dumped. Death on his hands, his life, over as he knew it. And, now, he's wondering what next.

He looks down the current of the water and sees a round object get smaller and smaller. The anger inside turns to fear and his heart pumps a different type of rhythm. His body, it shakes and in his mind, he replays the last few minutes.

He screams, then cries, then both at the same time while people passing by stare out the windows of their cars. One person honks while another yells out the window.

Ambiguous is an only child. He isn't used to losing attention. While society blames Ambiguous it really should take his parents into custody. Sometimes, parents with one child are the worst crime of them all. The lack of social skills? Sometimes it leads to illnesses. The mental abuse thinking that you can't do anything wrong? Sometimes it leads to identity confusion. Or paranoia.

One time, Ambiguous remembers, his cousin came over to visit. His mother asked him to share his toys, but instead of sharing, Ambiguous threw a fit and took all of his toys to his room. His mother, she forced him to leave one toy. But not just any toy, the favorite one. She said, "Sweetie, just until he goes home. Please, do this for me."

Ambiguous ensured an early departure by ripping the toy from his cousin's grasp and storming off into his room. The sharp scream by the cousin drew Ambiguous' mother to check in and upon arrival, discovered that the now favorite toy was cut up into a million pieces.

Ambiguous sat in the corner with his arms folded and pouted his lips. His mother, she called her sister and said, "Ambiguous isn't feeling well and I think it's best for you to pick up your son so he doesn't get sick."

A short talk about sharing was all that resulted from this behavior. And like parents of a single child, that behavior continued on until it was society's problem.

Ambiguous watches his child, falling helplessly until he could no longer see. This plays in his head over and over while he is being received into custody. The child, floating down the water looks just like his favorite toy, cut up into pieces so no one else can have it.

Ambiguous's wife, she's visiting the bridge on a regular basis, looking down into the river, saying a prayer over and over, while society around her, it forever reminds her of her reject husband. The news, copycat criminals, whenever a child turns up missing or dead, society sends a grave reminder.

Ambiguous, now in prison, draws back to his life before being locked up. His wife, his child, the one he murdered, the betrayal, all of it. His childhood is criticized by specialists on local news stations. Parents call in stating that it's hard to raise children when you're trying to make ends meet. They say, "Sometimes your child doesn't get the love and nurture he deserves. It's either let them fend for themselves or go hungry." The specialists, they say, "It's an ongoing problem for sure, but what are parents' options?"

An interview with Ambiguous' parents tell the tale of a good child turned bad due to society. "So many bad influences in our schools and on television," his mother says. She says, "He was always such a fine young man.

Sure, he got into trouble every now and then. But he's a kid."

Never in her wildest dreams did she think that her baby boy would ever turn out this way. She says this as she reinforces her parenting to reporters hoping to get another angle to this sordid story. "Don't blame the parents, we're doing the best we can."

And specialists, they're saying, "Even with all the programs available, when is a parent able to attend when she's busing working two jobs and making dinner for her family? And what about the costs of these programs? It certainly is an ongoing problem for sure."

Ambiguous sits in prison, thinking about how his wife found love in another man. He wonders why it was so easy for Unknown to get women. Ambiguous couldn't command his wife's attention, and Unknown, he's having women throw themselves at him. Ambiguous says, "Do you think women are that shallow when it comes to meeting a famous person?"

Unknown knows exactly why it was so easy for him to get women. He says, "Women love famous people. Something about being famous or knowing people who are famous. It's an attraction. It's attention they're not used to getting in their personal lives."

He says, "They see them as accomplished, like they've done something with themselves, when their own life sucks and is insignificant. They want to feel special just like everyone else."

Just like being anonymous, this works the other way. Instead of committing crimes to get noticed, they are making themselves noticed simply by rubbing noses with the ultimate noticed.

Women, how by being with the manager of Brad Pitt, being with the manager of Tom Cruise, being with the manager of Colin Farrell, they want something to hold over their friends whenever they see them, even if it isn't the stars themselves.

Society, it coddles you, it allows you to succeed. No child left behind, bankruptcy, it all results in people failing at real life. But don't worry, society will kiss your wound and tell you that everything will be all right. Just keep going out there and give it your best shot.

Unknown, he says, "They know there's no chance in hell they're going to end up with Brad Pitt. I was the closest thing to it."

It's like the band's manager who nails the excess groupies that strike out with the band members. Unknown says, "I was the same way. Something to give them to hold over their friends. Bragging rights. This person is accomplished." He says, "In their minds, now they're accomplished."

In their mind, these women who have failed in life, they've now achieved something that their friends can talk about. Society has a funny way of treating you, which is why, according to Unknown, the anonymous must keep it in check.

The fascination people have with celebrities is getting out of hand. Years ago, celebrity meant movie actors meant musicians meant athletes. People like Zsa Zsa Gabor, George Hamilton, and now Kim Kardashian, these are people famous for being famous. Now, celebrity, it's too vague.

Unknown says, "A local news personality, a celebrity. A car dealership owner selling cars on TV, a celebrity. Monica Lewinsky, she's a celebrity." He says, "For sucking the President's dick."

Unknown says, Shows like Entertainment Tonight and Extra, they're the tabloids of the television screen, something to keep celebrity in the minds of viewers. Did you see what so-and-so was eating this morning? This breakfast sandwich to the stars, it's now a must have food. Everyday folk orders it at his local diner and the cook is saying, "We don't make that here."

Some country diner, in a town of fewer than 100 people, the cook is being asked about a breakfast sandwich with tofu. "It's here in this magazine," a societal degenerate says, showing the picture of it to the staff. "Matt Damon is eating it."

"The tabloids are making celebrities feel important, above us, better than us." He says, "Just name drop someone like Arnold, and you're golden. It's infectious. It's a disease."

With anyone being famous, it opens up even more desperation to be like them. Unknown says, "Me included. I just took it a different way." Unknown says this to justify his actions. He says this because he believes it.

Voices come through the pipes by Ambiguous's toilet. A few of the prisoners, they drained out their toilets by using sponges and syringes and baling out the rest of the water. The prisoners are yelling back and forth through the drainpipes several times a day. Yelling back and forth, telling their own stories to each other. Stories about how one girlfriend used to spit and not swallow. Yeah, it's that kind of story.

The streaming voice says how the prisoner would scream at his girlfriend every time she did it. The voice, it says, "I told her time and time again, don't spit it out."

The voice, traveling through the drainpipes for all the inmates to hear, it's saying how he would eat fruit just so his come would taste sweeter. He says, "I hate fruit. Why the hell would I eat a banana and a pear?"

Ambiguous's cell, its six foot by nine foot slab of concrete, its stainless steel toilet, and the cot, its thin mattress makes for a bad experience. His toilet is still full but he can still hear voices clear. The voice, it's now saying how she finally swallowed and let's just say they didn't see each other much after that. The voice says, "But I ate the fruit."

The girl who likes sweet come, she read about this discovery in a women's magazine. "How to win over your man by swallowing your pride." A two page article with tips on how to make your man's love juice taste like a fruit smoothie when in real life it's anything but smooth. But here, in this leading publication, it states that this is the new thing that is going around tinsel town.

"Some A-list star, who wanted to remain nameless, likes to swallow it slowly because it reminds her of a melted banana shake," the article says.

There is laughter fading from the pipes and Ambiguous, he says, "I can't stay in this place. All those empty toilets, it's like the joke about having a dream about drinking the world's largest martini and then waking up and the toilet bowl is empty."

The voices are going back and forth through the world's largest martini glasses. One prisoner, his voice is saying how he doesn't like going down on a woman because his tongue hasn't gotten acquired to the taste.

Coming from the other way, the voice says, "Too bad. You're missing out man." Then, the voice says, "Spitting out. It offends me when a woman does that. It's not like I'm asking her to gargle for me. Just swallow it. I made it especially for you."

Sitting alone in his cell is Stud, listening to every story that rings through the drainpipes. He wants to tell his story, but is afraid of what others might think. So he waits, absorbing those tales that reach him, echoing through pipes, or those that are told by prisoners in cells adjacent to his.

One of the voices, through the drainpipes, it says, "I've been in love one time. It didn't last though." Ambiguous, annoyed with the conversation behind him, flushes the toilet.

Ambiguous's memory, it shuffles back to the time he first discovered his wife cheating on him. It was the look in her eyes. Baby blue ones, shaped like dimes. Eyelashes, thick, long and sexy. He says, "Her eyes, I caught them wandering one time."

Her eyes, they moved up and down this man's body, stopping every so often on his washboard stomach and defined arms. She says, "Honey, isn't that your friend Dave?"

Ambiguous looks at the man and shakes his head. It's not Dave. He says, "No, not even close." Then he smiles, his body shaking in laughter as if his wife is crazy. The man, not Dave, he's now catching Ambiguous' wife's eyes in a silent game of "I'm in the book, call me."

Instead of being crazy, his wife is being sneaky. She knows it isn't Dave. She knows by saying it's Dave is the only way she could cop a look, a long look.

She says, "You're right," looking at him one more time. "I'm in the book."

"I didn't think anything of it," Ambiguous says. "It wasn't until I caught them in bed together." His face, her lover's, it screamed not Dave. His wife, lying on her back, her eyes closed, her body weak, her legs buckled, it certainly wasn't Dave.

"Dave wouldn't have done this to me," he says.

The man, not Dave, he jumped from Ambiguous's wife, scared, mortified, in horror. He was saying, "Shit!" is all Ambiguous could remember. All this while their child slept in peace a few rooms down.

Ambiguous, he had one rage, one temper gone awry. The result was a murdered child, and now he's spending life in the slammer.

His wife visits the bridge regularly and says a prayer over and over, sometimes with not Dave and sometimes alone. All the time she's with a photograph, a toy truck or blankie that the child used to love.

His wife says about her husband, "His mother should have had an abortion. A coat hanger abortion."

Ambiguous trembles, he's contrite and sorry. And to anyone that asks, "Why didn't you kill him or the wife? Why the baby?" Ambiguous tells them it made him wonder if it was his. The paranoia was too much for him. The constant thinking the worse, it was too much.

The voices, behind him, they say back and forth, "Fruit so it tastes sweeter?" And, "I'm telling you, that's what some chick told me one time. Come tastes better depending on what the dude ate."

The voice, responding says, "I'm gonna take your word for it."

Society now has an Amber Alert Plan, for cases such as this. Ambiguous, his abducted child, the baby's abduction is broadcast everywhere like an incoming tornado, all thanks to little Amber Hagerman. Amber was riding her bike, enjoying the day, her life simple and innocent, when a man kidnapped her. The man tossed Amber into his truck and drove away. A neighbor, she phoned the police, giving her input, and a description of what she saw. She says, "I can't recall that much else." And days later, searches later, tears later, cries for help later, aided by TV and radio stations covering the case, Amber Hagerman was found less than a good walk away.

Amber, her throat was cut. Her case, it's still unsolved. There's now an Amber Alert Plan. And specialists, they're on the television saying, "Parents work sometimes three jobs to support their families. They can't watch their children all the time. It's an ongoing problem for sure."

Amber Alert, dedicated on locating and recovering children before something bad happens, before the Ambiguous's of the world happen, and now, it's nationwide. The Department of Justice reports that 5000 children are abducted every year. And right now, you're doing the math, figuring out how many children that are a day. That's something like thirteen kids a day. That's definitely an ongoing problem for sure.

What law will become of Ambiguous's action is anyone's guess. Or maybe they should just make the Amber Alert Plan better. Maybe they should name the plan after a case that has actually been solved. That's like the government saying, "Amber Alert? Your child will most certainly come up dead and we'll never find the killer. But thanks for playing along."

Faint voices zip through the pipes, only heard clear from certain cells, and in the other cells the voices sound like ghosts. The other prisoners, some reading, some letter writing and some watching television, some with their faces up to the bars, keep to themselves until the lights go out.

Stud, he listens to the conversations go in and out, his own story locked inside waiting to be released and judged. Unknown tells him that when he's ready, people will listen. These prisoners are one and the same, society's bottom of the barrel that hope to make a name for themselves.

Charlie Manson, he's a cult figure for conspiring to kill in the Tate/LaBianca murders. Although he never actually murdered anyone, he was found guilty through the joint-responsibility rule, a rule that holds each member equally accountable of crimes that fellow conspirators commit.

"These prisoners," Unknown says, "they're all equally accountable for their actions. Me included. This prison is one big cult. Like one big multiple personality disorder."

Behind Stud, through the drainpipes, voices are talking about blow jobs and swallowing. "What kind of fruit?" one says. It says, "Just bananas and pears?"

One of the voices, it says, "I like the frozen bananas."

One of the voices, it says, "I like caramel apples."

One of the voices, it says, "I like banana chips. Do those count? I'll eat the fuck out of those." The voices, they converse back and forth, killing time. They do this when they're feeling irrelevant. It's how they cope with their situations.

4.

You can always tell if a guy's psychotic because the first thing he'll tell you when he's asking you out is, "I'm not a psycho." The bad thing about being superficial is looks; what's on the outside always seem to make up for what's on the inside. What's on the inside really does count.

One really big nobody is only referred to as Nose around the cell block. Nose has got an extraordinarily big nose.

Nose says, "It wasn't always this big. I got into a couple fights and it just didn't heal right." His nose is crooked and one nostril is bigger than the other. It's been broken at least four times, once with a chair, twice with a fist, and a mishap involving his door at night. His nose, it's seen better days. His nose, always sticking its business where it shouldn't be. A snide comment about his girlfriend, bumping someone the wrong way, a quarrel with a loved one, his nose, it's always bumping into things.

Unknown, he says, "Give me Nose for one day and he becomes the legend of Owen Wilson." Owen Wilson, a big enough star to support Unknown's woman addiction. His popularity struggles. He does this when he's feeling irrelevant.

Nose is in prison for stalking his ex-girlfriend. He says, "I violated the restraining order she had on me. One hundred fucking yards." A football field's length, a mall parking lot, wherever she is, Nose can't be around.

Nose, a symbolic name because he knows everywhere his ex-girlfriend is, day and night. "That," Ambiguous says, "and you have a big nose."

Nose says, "I told you, it wasn't always this big."

The ghosts in the pipes, one says, "I used to date this woman. The only problem I had with her was her honker for a nose. After a while though, I didn't notice it as much."

Unknown tells Nose that his girlfriend wasn't giving him her full attention. He says, "You gave her everything and then some, and in return, she gets a restraining order on you?"

"All you wanted," Unknown says, "was to be wanted, to feel important. She didn't give that to you. Instead, what she gave you was a football field long barrier."

Now, whenever ex-boyfriends appear in places they shouldn't be, they're hauled down to the station. Thank you society, thank you very much. This is society's way of putting you in a corner. This is your parents' way of saying, "Just don't talk to that boy anymore. Find some other friends."

Going out to a bar to have a couple drinks and by chance your ex is there, sitting on a bar stool talking to some guy. The pure coincidence violates the restraining order. There's one more establishment your presence isn't wanted.

Nose's insecurity stems from his childhood. His mother had no idea who Nose's father was. And she didn't care. But whenever Nose asked, she would say, "You don't need him," and "We're much better off without him."

Nose took care of himself with his mother gone most of the time. She said she would be home by dinner and the next thing Nose knew was he was fixing breakfast for himself. When he returned from school, his mother, Nose's mother, had an extravagant excuse and her eyes were bugged out and red.

Nose, about his ex-girlfriend, says, "Right now, she's on her way to work, driving on 23rd Avenue. She used to call me while she drove. I'd talk to her until she got to work." Mostly Nose and his girlfriend would talk about nothing important, maybe dinner that night and what movie she should pick up. He says, "But it didn't make a difference. As long as we were talking."

Nose's childhood, waiting for his mother to come home, trusting her every word, giving her the benefit of the doubt, it's what got him trouble with his ex. The worrying that Nose's ex wouldn't call, or show up when expected, the constant text messages and thinking the worst, the paranoia, it's a coping mechanism for Nose.

"One time," he says, "traffic was backed up for miles and we just sat, talking to each other, enjoying each other's company. Now, my company can only be enjoyed no closer than one hundred yards."

The paranoia, it became a co-morbidity in the form of depression, in the form of personality disorder. Are Nose's traits normal if that's all he's ever known?

The voice in the pipes, the other one, it says, "You didn't notice her big nose as much because you finally got used to it?"

The voice, once dating a woman with a honker for a nose, says, "No, she ended up putting on like fifty pounds. After that, it didn't look so big."

To anyone that asks the question, "What happened between you two?" Nose says, "Just like that, she decides that things just aren't working out. She says, 'It's not you, it's me.'" And me, it translates into Nose's head, that she's interested in seeing someone else.

He says, "What did I do? Is it something I did?" Memories from every little tense situation appear in his head, and he plays out the dialog for clues. He says, "Seriously, did I do something?"

The way Nose talks, it's as if he is a child again asking his mother why she's screaming. She shows up high and her speech is slurring and Nose, he's saying, "Momma, where were you? Why didn't you come home last night?"

Nose has no idea, but the bail out excuse of being told that it's not him, it's her, is well received until the next time she doesn't show up.

Nose's ex, she shakes her head, never looking Nose in the eyes, and unemotional tears, they fall down her cheek until she has his blessing that she just needs time to think things through. He says, "Take all the time you need," as his mind shifts from the time they were at the rock concert to the time they were watching fireworks at the park to the time his mother strolled in with some random stranger at three in the morning after promising she'd return with an ice cream cone.

His mother, she says, "Baby, I'll get you some ice cream. I just need to talk to my friend. We'll be in my room, OK? Don't bother us until we're done talking."

Nose agrees to give his ex time, and just like the incidents with his mother, his ice cream cone never comes.

Several television programs and multiple meals pass. Visits from friends and work shifts, they pass, all this while Nose is calling every day and every hour. When the credits roll and the station identification comes on the screen, he calls just to say hi and to see if she needs anything, anything at all.

He says, "Call me later, to tell me how things are going if anything." Her voice mail, there are tons of messages from Nose similar to this. His messages, they say, "Was thinking about you when I was at the deli buying a sandwich. I remember the time they screwed up your order. Just thought I'd share that with you. Well, just give me a call whenever." Then he hangs up and finds another memory of her to share.

Driving on 23rd Avenue, he knows when she's on it. Nose says, "I know her schedule by heart." A guy, you can tell he's psychotic because the first thing he'll tell you when he's asking you out is, "I'm not a psycho."

And just like with his mother, Nose gives his ex the benefit of the doubt.

Nose, he says, to himself, to his friends, to anyone, "She'll call me eventually." His friends are telling him, "Just be there for her. If she needs to talk, just listen to her."

His friends say, "She's confused. She doesn't know what she wants."

All the while her friends are telling him, "It's not like she's going out with other guys." Her friends, they hang up with him and then relay back the information to his ex, their friend. All the while his ex is saying, "There's this guy I've been talking to." In between the messages from Nose about how he saw a car that looked like her's are conversations with this guy she's been talking to.

And the days go by that her friends lie to him for her, saying that she's just been going to work and then coming home, but every once in a while, they say, she goes out with them and they get her drunk. They say, "You know, sometimes she needs to unwind."

His ex, she's saying to her friends, "This guy I've been talking to. It's now going somewhere." And her voice mail, there are tons of messages from Nose, saying if she needs to talk then call him.

But in reality, she's seeing some other guy who is better looking and has more money. Unknown tells Nose, "Nice guys finish last."

And Ambiguous says, "One with an unbroken nose."

And the ghosts say back and forth, "A big nose one day, then it's not so big anymore." And, "Weight, it's what changes a life. Pain, it's what changes a life." The ghost in the drainpipes, through the empty toilet bowl, says, "It was painful to look at her, knowing that she was once thin and now she's not."

Stud, on the other hand, flushes his toilet. When he does this, he misses out on certain parts of the story. At first the words are slushy, like a ventriloquist talking while drinking water.

"Who cares now? You're locked up in here." The drainpipes, they become quiet. Then Stud's toilet fills with water and the stories continue. Stud hasn't yet bailed out the water in his bowl. He's still waiting for the right time to tell his story.

This fear, it's what keeps Stud from being personable. Whenever he gets the urge to speak, his body, it suffers frequent panic and anxiety attacks. Even though no one can see him, it is the thought that he won't get the approval he is looking for.

Nose says, "I found out she was seeing someone else because I saw her driving and in the passenger seat, there was a guy. I followed them a few blocks, until I saw them stop at a light and lean into one another and kiss."

Her friends, they keep telling Nose that every once in a while they take her out to get her drunk. And that she doesn't do anything but work and sleep.

Nose says, "I became obsessed, more like pissed, and eventually, I kept tabs on her, watching her do one thing while her friends tell me something different."

"I don't know where she's at," her friends say, "she's been working a lot lately." Her friends, they're starting to avoid Nose because the phone calls become more frequent. Their voice mails, they're filled with messages from Nose asking about their friend, wondering how she is doing.

Nose's messages become shorter and shorter and the anger can be heard through the machine. His ex-girlfriend, she's telling her friends to stop answering, to change their numbers or to see about taking out a restraining order themselves.

She says, "Seriously, it's not worth it to talk to him."

Nose, into the bowl, he says, "You know how I got caught? She caught me outside three places she was at and I didn't have an excuse why I was there. The next thing I know, a fucking restraining order. One hundred mother fucking yards."

Nose says, "One of the places, it was a salon. Dead giveaway."

Her voice mail, there are no more messages from Nose. None that say, "Call me." None that say, "I miss you." None that say, "How's work?" None of that. One contact, one communication, via restraining order.

"A salon," Nose says, "dead giveaway."

Nose, restraining order-type A, making girls feel safer in public places since 2006. Stalking girls has just gotten harder. A voice in the pipes, some random voice that is unrecognizable to the regular crew, begins to tell a story, dedicated to Nose.

This story, it's about a stalker whose mission is to make girls think twice about people they don't know. This story, it travels through the drains, at flushing speed, and in some inmates' cells, it sounds like a ghost.

Stud closes his eyes and enjoys. The water in his toilet bowl is calm. There is not a single ripple that interrupts this story.

5.

Emily is a short haired vixen with blond, almost white spiky hair. She has a small nose stud exiting from her left nostril sparkling like a star in the sky, and everyday, she can't help but look over her shoulder.

Her ex-boyfriend, or psycho as Emily refers to him, stalks her. Behind his tinted window and through the windshield of his car, he's there. She says, "He's always there, I can feel him. Every once in a while, I'll get goose bumps. All from a feeling."

The two, they dated for a couple weeks, but after five phone calls within an episode of Sex And The City, Emily says, "That's nuts." She says, "The messages, they'd say things like, 'I guess you don't like me anymore,' stuff like that."

Messages, left one after the other, all saying things that relay insecurity to Emily, and she's now saying it was a mistake to have given him her number.

Emily says about him, "You can always tell if a guy is psychotic because the first thing he'll tell you when he's asking you out is, 'I'm not a psycho.'"

This line, at first, Emily thought it was cute. She hasn't dated in a while and that sense of humor, well, to Emily it seemed harmless. Being single for a while, it does stuff to your brain. Want to know a way to get laid? Ask out the girl who hasn't had a boyfriend for years. You know which one she is in her group of friends. She's the one that doesn't try as much. She's the one that gets a low maintenance haircut so she can still look cute with very little work. Or the girl who gets a piercing in her nose so she can still wear jewelry without any effort. She's the one that looks great without makeup or dressed down.

Emily, she's a bartender at a fancy hotel. Her ex, he comes in and sits at the bar, drinking. This is well after the successive phone calls, well after the days and then weeks of ill communication.

He says, "I'm just waiting for a friend who's staying here." Emily knows this is a lie because he sits there, waiting, for glasses and glasses of draft beer and then disappearances to the bathroom and finally, he leaves, only to sit in his vehicle until Emily exits the hotel door. All this while Emily is wishing the hotel has security.

Her ex, sitting in his car, binoculars in hand and the darkness, it is hindering his ability to catch a glimpse of the facial expressions and gestures that Emily exerts to no one in particular as she heads for her car en route to God knows where.

Emily's destination is anywhere she can get the thoughts of her psychotic ex she now regrets whole heartedly of going out with. Almost to her car, her ex, he says with his binoculars in position, "I see you." His voice, it's raspy and soft, almost soft enough where he can't even hear what he's saying.

If you could see his eyes through the lenses, you'd swear they were in a state of trance. They don't blink and his focus is glaring. It's like he's in a different universe.

He says, "Where are we going out to tonight?" as he flips on his dimmers and shifts into drive, a couple blocks behind Emily.

Emily drives to a bar just a few miles away from her home, to meet a girlfriend who is so glad she finally smartened up and dumped that stalker, and the two, they're ordering shots, one at a time until they've got a good enough buzz for Emily to forget about him.

But, behind her, at a table in the distance, separated by bodies of bar patrons, clouds of spray perfume, smoke puffs blowing out from people's lips, he's staring, gawking, watching, and obsessing.

His hand, his right one, is closed in a fist as it dives into his front pant pocket. It pets himself until he reaches full potential. He does this as the waitress asks if he needs something to drink. He says, "Just a rum and Coke," while his fist grazes his penis until it hardens, until the inner denim is damp enough for him to go home satisfied.

His closed hand, hidden under the round table, his body's deep breathing, it's the only thing that could give him away.

Emily, having a blast with her friend, drinking it up as her girlfriend calls it, says, "He came into my work tonight. The fucker came into my work and just sat there."

Her friend says, "You need to get a restraining order on him." And the two down another shot, the sixth one so far, the empty glasses lined up in front of them in a row.

"We should stalk him," Emily says. She says, "Wouldn't that be a hoot?"

After a couple more drinks, her body feeling more and more relaxed, as if she knows her ex is gone from the premises, Emily raises her shot glass and says, "To stalking my ex. Give him a taste of his own medicine."

This is how Emily and her friend, Laura, toast, "Stalk the stalker," and then they laugh and clank their glasses. Around them, the bar is filled with party goers. Some could be stalkers, Christians, people cheating on their spouses, or convicts. But the only person that Emily gives a shit about is her stalker ex-boyfriend.

Her ex, he's now laying in bed, with his body breathing heavy. The picture of Emily taped to one of the posts of his four poster bed, the bed he uses to imaginary violate Emily, its image is smiling back at him.

Emily and Laura say, "Let him feel what it's like to be stalked. The creepiness, the constant looking around, wondering if he's there, in the shadows ducking down under his steering wheel, and behind the bush that's in front of the apartment building."

Emily says, "He said he was waiting for a friend who had a room there. And of course, no one showed. Who the hell sits at the bar waiting for their friend? Just go up to the damn room."

"Did you tell your boss?" Laura says, looking around the bar to see if Emily's ex is anywhere to be found. She says, "I'm surprised he's not here now."

Emily turns and stares at the faces that surround her. One by one, she's looking at their eyes, as if he's somehow transformed into a heavy set woman with spandex, a junior college educated teen with a fake ID, or a blue collar, callus skinned man with a long beard. She says, "Yeah, no kidding."

A few feet away from them, a table is being cleared by the waitress, a single glass with dark liquid basing the bottom of it. She walks by Emily and Laura, the glass in her fingers and asks the two if they need anything else.

Laura says, "What was in there?" referring to the glass cupped in the waitress's hand.

The waitress, looking into the glass, says, "Rum and Coke."

Emily and Laura, they both look to each other, and then to the server, and say, "Rum and Coke it is."

Her ex, he's masturbating with one hand while holding the picture of Emily in the other. The picture is of Emily at a family reunion. She gave the photo to him because he told her how cute she looked in it.

The two, they're placing the glasses in a row, twelve of them now, and the waitress is coming back with their rum and Cokes. She says, "Eight dollars," and pulls out her leather pamphlet of loose bills and bar napkins.
Laura says, handing over a ten, "Keep the change."

They clank the drinks, with Laura's drink spilling over the rim, and Emily says, "The stalker will be stalked." They chug the beverages until the glasses are empty.

Laura licks the spilt drink from her thumb and finger, and says, "Stalk the stalker. Woot!"

"Tomorrow," Emily says. "Tomorrow, he'll be at work. We'll sit in the car, watching him through the window of the body shop."

They order one more drink and Emily says, "I'll call you tomorrow."

The next day, Emily and Laura hide out in Emily's car just outside her ex-boyfriend's work.
In the parking lot of the shop, the sun is shining through the windshield and the sauna-like heat is rising, forcing Emily to roll down her window. She says, "There's his car, but I don't see him."

His car, a 1980 Monte Carlo, sits alone in the parking lot across the street, the designated place were employees park. The closest car to his is half a lot away.

Emily says, "I wonder why he parks so far from everyone. It's not like he's got a nice car."

Laura, she says, "Because he's crazy. That's what crazy people do. They don't do anything normal. If he were normal, he'd park next to everyone else."

Emily shakes her head and says, "Fucking psycho."

Laura moves her head, left to right, until the ex appears in sight. "There he is," she says. The two stare, gawking at him, hoping to make him feel uncomfortable like Emily does. The feeling of his skin tightening and goose bumps forming, the thought of being watched. "Shivers," Emily says, "that's what it feels like."

Emily says, "I can't believe I went out with him. What a fucking freak." They watch for a few seconds and Emily says, "Duck down, he's coming out."

Her ex exits the shop and runs to his car, and sits. The window creeps down and the girls see him light up a cigarette, his left arm flying out the window with a lit Marlboro in his fingers. Through the back window, Emily sees her ex, the stalker, rest his head back.

Through her binoculars, Laura, she sees the ex, the stalker, through his rear view mirror. His mouth, it's open and dry, and his eyes, they're closed and every so often, he takes a drag of his cigarette. Small puffs of smoke exit his mouth and make the car slightly foggy for the details of what is going on to be clear.

Emily says, "Let's go." She opens the door slowly, and Laura, her position still behind the binoculars, looks a little longer until she loses the binoculars on the back seat.

Laura follows Emily, with the two walking very softly on the concrete, sneaking in a way the ex would do or probably does at night, until they reach the rear bumper of his car.

Her ex is relaxing, music coming out of his cheap, factory speakers, with his one arm out the window and his head back, eyes closed. His right arm, it's unseen to the two girls as they move closer to his door.

The car, it starts to squeak and grunts escape his mouth. Faint puffs of smoke appear as half circles as the grunts get louder. Emily cuts a look to Laura, and says, "What is he doing?"

Laura, copping a peek through his side mirror, says, "Don't know. I don't know."

The car shakes a little harder. The squeaks are a little louder and finally, finally, after a few more grunts, the windshield, it gets splattered with a shot of come that looks like bird crap.

"Gross," Emily says, in a stern whisper. She says, "Fucking gross." Before they can move, the door opens. "Shit," she says, and Emily and Laura slither around to the passenger side of the car.

Her ex, his left foot appears and hits the gravel, followed by his other foot. The girls duck underneath the passenger side door. The driver's side door slams and they hear footsteps walk away from them, farther until they're quiet enough to look.

Extending her body, Emily looks into the passenger side window. On the console, a picture, the picture once taped to his bed, shakes her back into her skin.

Emily, she says, "That the picture I gave him from my family reunion."

Next to it, candids of Emily walking to her car from work, sitting on her couch taken from the street peering into the window, enjoying lunch on a patio of some sports bar, they're all making Emily light headed and shaky. The same feeling she has whenever he's out there, watching her, gawking at her, staring at her, with those eyes, those crazy eyes. The feeling, it's hitting her again, this time ten thousand times harder.

"That's you," Laura says, joining her friend as they peer into the window. The windshield, it's now stained with DNA and the girls are saying they should have never decided to do this. Laura, she says, "Those are pictures of you."

Emily, she's shaking her head and her body is now feeling worse than any time she's been stalked by him. Emily says, "This fucking guy is crazy."

Laura is making a face. She is wanting to throw up, right there next to his car, but nothing wants to come out. She says, "You need to get a restraining order. Seriously, this isn't funny anymore."

The girls disappear from the area and Emily complies with Laura's request, a restraining order. But every now and then, her body, Emily's body, it shakes for no reason. It tenses up, her skin tightens, and goose bumps form when it's not cold. It regains the feeling that she's being watched, being photographed, and being violated.

She says, "I should've never given him my number. Psycho."

All the while Nose is saying, "She's now driving down Harrison Street. She's now driving down Locust Street. She's now driving up Main Street."

His ex, more and more she's turning her head to look behind her to see if anyone is there. And every time, there's nobody.

Nose, he knows everywhere his ex-girlfriend is.

6.

Things are never what they seem to be. Unknown says, "First impressions are important. That's why people pay so much attention to the latest fads and trends. Whatever it is, if you're hip and trendy, you're in."

Unknown, he's in prison for deception. He's in prison for fraud. He's in prison for trademark infringement. And all because he feels irrelevant. And all because he's a nobody.

Think about it. Think of all the ex-convicts out of prison, roaming the world with innocent people. When they're at the grocery store or mall, no one sees felon or criminal. Unknown says, "People, they see someone who needs a haircut, someone who needs a new shirt, or someone who needs braces."

When a person is arrested for being a pedophile, the neighbors, those poor neighbors, they say, "He was always so kind. He'd never do something like that. I guess you never know, do you?"

All this while he's being hauled away in handcuffs and media people are capturing every second of his arrest. Neighbors, bystanders, they're hugging each other and shaking their heads. "He would always be outside gardening," a woman says. She says, "My kids would talk to him every day." And now, the woman's kids are in therapy and giving statements to the police to put this man away.

Who knows what the long term effect will be? Who knows how these kids will "cope" with their lives?

Some of the victims, the ones that don't come forward because they're embarrassed at how they will be looked at, they develop coping mechanisms as they grow older. This sexual child abuse, imposed by a pedophile living in the neighborhood, is the only crime that this criminal will face.

And now, the abused will have to go an eternity dealing with past memories of a neighbor gone bad. All because they are too embarrassed to have been touched in their naughty places. Their experiences will show up in future relationships and the recipient, he or she will blame something other than a convicted child toucher rotting in prison until he gets paroled.

This man, a pedophile behind closed doors, he is not a nobody anymore. If anything, anything at all, he's making people more aware of quote unquote normal looking people.

This child toucher, Tex, is the master of all pedophiles. He's now in prison, caught for picking up children in Internet chat rooms. He's middle aged, his hairline is receding on the sides of his head, and the rest of his hair is thinning. Black roots that go into a light gray, his age is showing fifty.

Online, however, he's any age you want him to be.

Online, he's any weight you want him to be.

And online, he's any one you want him to be.

That cool kid from New York that is going to come visit this summer, well, he actually will be in town this weekend. And that's not all, he got a hotel room with an indoor pool. But don't tell your mother because, well, just don't. OK?

What has two thumbs and front row seats to The Jonas Brothers concert? This guy, but don't tell your mother because, well, just don't. OK?

Who wants to sit in a hotel room naked and watch movies all night while eating junk food until we puke? But don't tell your mother because, well, just don't. OK?

His face, it's wrinkled around his eyes, and his lips, what he has for lips, they're like a chicken's and point outward a half inch. The wrinkles on his face, they're like rails as they've been existent for much of his adult life. His pointy chin and high cheek bones, it's a wonder why he had to pick up dates online. His dry skin and cracked lips, it's a wonder why he had to pick up dates online.

He says, "A cop posing as a ten year old got me." The man, only known by the inmates as Tex, says, "When I got to the hotel parking lot, they were waiting for me. It was like a scene from Cops."

Before Tex could shift his car into park, it was surrounded with men showing badges. "The glare from the badges," Tex says, "they were so close I could read the lettering. I'll never forget that day. A car zoomed in behind me, blocking any chance of me escaping."

In the trunk of his car, Tex had board games, children's movies, candy and, oh by the way, condoms, lubrication and masking tape for good measure. To the cops, Tex says, "Those items are my son's. I don't know what he was using them for."

The cops yanked Tex out of his car, bagged the evidence, and threw him in the back seat of the police car. All the while the boy's parents were watching from another official's vehicle, crying to themselves wondering where they went wrong.

This pedophile picking up children online, parents are now writing to their congressman to get the Internet regulated. Signatures upon signatures sign a petition made up by a group of mothers hoping that something will be done to prevent future Tex's.

Tex, he's tall and lanky, and his prison jumpsuit is baggy around his body. The back of him is perfectly straight. There are no shoulder blades, no butt cheeks, and no calves. He hasn't seen a gym in years.

He says, "I've picked up three kids on the Internet. All of them were legit." This is what his police file says. Word for word. All of them were legit. Now, the cops are looking into these cases.

One of these children, he's now coping with life by finding a happy place and losing himself in it. His parents think he's daydreaming; psychiatrists worry that it could be something more.

"When it rains, it pours," Tex says, his life looking more and more bleak as he awaits trial. Tex, he's in custody and is the newest addition to Unknown's world.

Tex, a symbolic name for picking up children on the Internet. His text is Comic Sans.

Unknown says, "Maybe you wanted to get caught." He says, "Hiding behind that computer screen, with no one knowing who you are."

Tex, he just wants to belong. With someone, with society, something to take himself out of his invisible existence. What he doesn't know is he does belong. He's on the Internet. Just type in that website that tells you all the pedophiles in your neighborhood and those who are in custody. His picture is next to some guy who looks like your neighbor, above some guy who looks like your doctor, and below some guy who looks like your cousin. If a person mistakenly found this website, the initial thought would be, "some sort of YMCA basketball league." But the reality tells anyone who logs on. "Do you know where your children are?" And "Do you really know your neighbors?"

Tex used to be a janitor at an elementary school. At night, he's the only one in there. He whistles because the silence is too eerie for him. He talks to himself, often engaging in conversations that extend beyond the ones he finds himself in during the course of the day.

These conversations, although in his head, are far too real for Tex. "Hi Annie," he says, "what's for lunch today?" Annie, she's got a lifetime of experiences ahead of her, cute as a button. Her dimples, they're huge because her cheeks are so big. Her smile, it's what gets Tex.

"Tex," he says, "The good thing about being a pedophile is their little hands make your dick look huge."

Tex says to Annie in the hall, "What's for lunch today?"

Annie, she can say anything at this time, hot-dogs, pizza, hamburgers. To Tex, however, it comes out, molestation, feeling up, bloody vagina.

Annie, she says, "Milk, and fruit, and..." She pauses with her lips puckered, her finger tapping her bottom lip trying to think of what else is on the menu. "Um, and apples." She smiles at Tex, her two front teeth missing.

Tex, he hears, "Baby soft skin. No pubes," as he mentally dreams of something sliding in between her gapped teeth.

"Do you like apples?" Annie says to Tex.

Tex, his eyes locked on Annie's, says, "I do. Thank you for asking." He says, "Do you like magic?"

Annie smiles and nods her head at the same time. Tex says, "Maybe I can show you a trick later." She smiles and nods her head. Tex says, "Just come see me after school and I'll show you one." Annie laughs and then turns to rejoin her class in line. She looks back at Tex and waves by opening and closing her fingers.

After a while, it drives Tex mad. He says, "It's not acceptable."

But every night, he cleans the halls, mopping and pushing the big, plastic yellow bucket with soapy water. He walks the halls, seeing pictures drawn by little Annie, little Rebecca, and little Ambrosia. Tex, he sees construction paper projects with excess glue escaping from the bottom of paper arms or legs. There's a self portrait, by Carrie Young.

Tex pulls off a self-portrait, this one by Lori S. The tape, one strand is stuck on the back of the paper, the other is stuck on the brick wall. He holds the portrait up in front of him, and from there, Tex drops his pants and masturbates to Lori S.

On the front, the artwork is sloppy with the eyes not lined up right. The nose is crooked and the smile is too large for the face. Each eye is a different color and the teeth have purple gaps in between.

The ghosts in the pipes, they sound like the empty halls' echoes whenever Tex yells something out. He says, "Hello, hello," and hears, "hello, hello." The voices in the drainpipes, they're as if Tex is hearing himself.

Lori S.'s self-portrait, it's held up by Tex's hand while he pleasures himself. The mess, the school officials can't explain it. The picture, the self portrait, it looks like glue on Lori's face. Lori S., her moon-like smile, cut from a piece of red construction paper, smiles as glue, or egg, or something, violates her eyes and hair. The purple in between the teeth have a white, sticky substance as if Lori S. is eating melted marshmallow.

Lori, she cries, and the teacher is letting her redo her assignment.

The substance is sniffed by several teachers and the principal. They have no idea what it is. Elmer's glue, possibly. An egg? Who knows? DNA, not a chance.

This is why Tex is here, in prison. He blames loneliness. And Tex, he says, to anyone that will listen, "Their badges were so close I could read them. I'll never forget that day."

Tex has forgotten a lot of things in his life, even some of the intimate details that police officers have said he has committed. But the one thing he'll never forget are the badges.

The ghosts in the drainpipes are talking about how lonely it is in the cell. The TV programs airing, they are becoming realer and realer every day and the video games, they are becoming more lifelike with every level played.

Stud is sitting on the toilet doing his business while gargling voices are escaping from under his ass.

There's another self-portrait, put together with corn kernels for teeth, glued together like a boomerang. Her smile is long and wide. Her eyes, they're two pennies and her nose is a Dots candy. Tex, he says, "I love Dots." And the school officials are wondering what the stained yellow stuff is plastered up and down her cheek. A portrait, by Annabelle G. DNA, by Tex. Her teacher is now letting her redo the assignment.

Tex, he blames loneliness. As a child, Tex was always by himself. His mother wouldn't let friends come over, partly because she didn't want anyone to know that every Thursday, Tex had to perform for his mother.

Tex thought he was just role playing, stripping down to his underwear and prancing around the living room until his mother forced him to show her his wiener. "Come here, son, let me pull on it," she said to him.

Tex, laughing and playing, all the joy in the world, with complete trust in his mother, lets his mother fondle him until it feels too good to stop. Every Thursday, Tex looks forward to play time with mommy.

Tex, now in prison, wonders why he is like this. Not a family member comes to visit, especially his mother.

Unknown is saying that society needs people like Tex, like himself because now, the sex offender's registry is available online. Just go to a website, put in a person's name and you can see if one of your neighbors has been arrested for a sex related crime. Without the Tex's, Unknown says, these sex offenders will be unaccounted for.

They would be unknown. They would be anonymous. They would be the mailman. They would be the door to door salesmen. Just when you think you're hiding from a Jehovah's Witness, you're really ducking down behind the couch from James, the twice convicted child toucher.

Unknown says, "Tex matters now." Society has Tex to thank for being able to track pedophiles now. Your neighbors, they have Tex to thank for being able to track sex offenders now.

Unknown, he says, "Go forward with the lemonade stands, macaroni art galleries and hopscotch, because now you can find out if your neighbor is a sex offender."

Megan's Law, it's society's answer to the Tex's of the world. Brochures, they ask, What does Megan's Law mean to you? PSA's, billboards, magazine articles, they all tell you that in 1994, Megan Kanka disappeared. Megan was lured from her home to her neighbor's house. A place that, to the rest of the residents on the block, was a couple houses down or in the neighborhood or the house with a lawn sprinkler always going off. A place that, to Megan, was her last day of breathing. A place where she was raped, strangled and suffocated.

While the horror went on inside behind closed curtains, pedestrians walking by were commenting to each other that this guy needed to cut the grass.

Megan's Law, it's because after her murder, she was stuffed into a toy box and dumped in a city park. PSA's, billboards, magazine articles, they tell you that Megan's perpetrator was a twice convicted child offender who lived in a house in Megan's neighborhood. He lived in the house with other convicted sex offenders. And you can bet that, once this information was made known, people were saying, "We'd be better off if people in the Witness Protection Program lived on our block."

Megan, lured into a house where she was raped.

Megan, strangled, suffocated and then dumped in a park.

Megan, thanks to her case, there's a Megan's Law.

Megan's Law, it forces convicted child offenders to register with local police departments. So that neighbors will know if a child lover is living among them. They may not like it, but at least they know. But this isn't what upsets them. What upsets them is that parents don't even get this information all the time because police departments have small budgets, and well, you can guess how this might be a problem.

All Stud is thinking right now is that he knows a Megan. He thinks this as he drops a deuce in the bowl.

Thanks to the Tex's in the world, there's now a National Alert Registry. Anyone can get on a computer and do a search, entering general information, to see if the guy next door is a pedophile. And Unknown, he's saying how society needs people like him, people like them.

Unknown says, "Take the bank robber, he's taking money, not only for his own purpose, but so people know about him. So people are aware of him."

The lookout is for a man, medium build, about 5 feet 10 inches tall, weight approximately 180 pounds, Caucasian, considered armed and dangerous. The description, this is what gets the bank robber excited.

The attention, it's what gets the bank robber excited.

The images on the television, the cop's statement to the reporter on the scene, it's why the robber robbed. There's looped footage of a grainy picture showing the man taking the money and turning, taking the money and turning, and then finally moving out of view. The bank robber can't get enough of it.

Before the heist, the criminal was a regular Joe with a regular job, non-existent to his co-workers. He collected and distributed mail in a bank, the same bank he robbed, delivering and sorting letters and correspondences to loan officers, bankers, accountants and secretaries. All of which went unnoticed.

"Not a thank you," he says. "They didn't even know my name." This is what he says at his trial. Delivering packages, letters, brown manila envelopes, all this while the bankers, loan officers and accountants are typing away on computers and chatting on their telephones. "Not one thank you," he says.

The rest of the prisoners, they don't know his real name but they call him Steele, a symbolic name because he left the bank with $19,000 dollars.

Unknown says, "They know your name now." And you can bet the employees will think of him anytime the bank's new mail person shows up with letters.

"Hi Larry," the loan accountants say, making it a point to stop whatever it is they are doing. "How is your day, today? It sure is a wonderful day." They're protecting themselves from future Steele's. This is how he matters now.

The bank now holds mandatory introductory meetings, a "get to know your fellow colleague" meeting, with punch and cupcakes and games that explore the employees' sillier sides.

"I love trivia games," and then a swallow of punch. "I love knitting," and then a handful of Skittles. One woman is president of an actor's fan club, and then playful laughter. She says, "You get a signed eight by ten and a membership card." These introductory meetings, they are all courtesy of Steele. Steele says, "They didn't even know my name."

Steele loves trivia games, knitting to him is just fine as long as he's not doing it, and he says, "That actor plays in good movies." Steele, he loves candy, he loves cupcakes, and punch, well, it's fine too. But Steele, locked up, says, "They didn't even know my name."

Steele was caught with bags of money, sitting in his house staring at the bills and then to the newscast. "The lookout is for a..."

"I guess you never know about a person." This is the word in the neighborhood as people watch these normal nobody's being hauled away in cuffs. Now they're looking at each other more cynically.

The next time you see a normal person, don't be surprised if they turn out to be a wee bit different. Don't be surprised if their silence is a way of coping with something they really don't want anyone to know about. You can Google images all you want, using different key words and your zip code, but the difference with what you find and what you don't is these people just haven't gotten caught yet.

This is a story about a normal person who, you guessed it, is a wee bit different, told by a voice, some random voice, some anonymous voice.

7.

Swingers are gross, they're always ugly people. But the idea of sleeping with a married man, she says, that's so trendy. You are so hip.

The two women sit in the non-smoking section of a restaurant, making a day of it as both their husbands are out doing whatever with whomever. Patrons of the like, as seen by the two women, they sit and eat their respective meals, some hot, some cold and some that just don't look right. "This isn't what I ordered," a nearby woman says to her server.

The swinger, now a concerned Christian, Tiffany, says she stopped playing the game because her throat, well, it just couldn't take it anymore.

Her friend, she says, "Having an affair, it seems that everyone is doing it today." She says, to her born again religious, once upon a time out of control pole sucker, "I'm so jealous." She says how her husband, if she ever dared cheat on him, he'd kill her. "Seriously," she says, "he'd kill me without a hesitation. It doesn't matter if it's kissing, having sex, or sucking pole, he won't put up with it."

The women, they like to sit in the non-smoking section because, according to them, it's the only thing people can tell about them - non-smokers. On the outside,

Tiffany and her friend, they're two regular women with regular jobs and regular chores.

Tiffany's car is parked outside and if you tried guessing which one belonged to her, you'd be way off.

The Toyota Camry with the Jesus fish on the back?

The mini-van with the family static sticker?

The sporty Nissan Maxima with the tinted windows?

Or D, none of the above?

Tiffany is a Nurse Practitioner for an Army clinic base. On the arsenal, Tiffany, she sees patients and diagnoses family members. All of her efforts are geared toward assisting the American soldier and his family.

When friends find out she works for the government, they say, "Is it just like the stereotype? Government workers are lazy?"

Tiffany, she wishes that is the only problem.

In between patients, looking outside her window, watching the soldiers raise and salute the flag, all for a country that is free, brave and stands for something, Tiffany steals medicine to soothe the pain in her throat. Her throat, it just can't take it anymore.

Now, if someone sees Tiffany and her friend, they think, "Non-smokers."

The conversation between them, now down to whispers and frequent looks over each other's shoulder, it tells a different story.

Tiffany, she's not so trendy anymore. After years of sucking the pole, as she calls giving head, she says, "I had to stop because of the constant infections I was getting in my throat."

Tiffany says, Iugulan Neisseria Gonorrhea.

Tiffany says, It's a venereal disease.

Tiffany says, Only it breaks out in your throat.

"Throat clap," she says, "I had to stop because it was getting out of hand." Her friend thinks swingers are gross. She says they're always ugly people. And now Tiffany says swingers have diseases too. She says, "My husband has diseases too. It's not worth it. It's just not worth it."

A table of suits next to them, they're drinking beer and having a good time. Rows of empty glasses wait to be picked up. Empty plates with half eaten appetizers are scattered around the table. The group just landed a big account for the company it works for.

One suit says, "Another round, on me." A couple men, they raise their glasses and each swallows the remains of what's inside his glass.

Tiffany turns around to look at them. Her face winces at the men swallowing. The movement of their Adam's apples, it's a constant reminder of how she used to take it. The gulping noise echoes in Tiffany's brain, putting her in a trance that is so spontaneous, she draws attention to herself.

Her friend, she says, "Tiffany? Is everything all right?"

A suit, he smiles at Tiffany and winks. This wink, it's like a hypnotist snapping his finger, and instantly, Tiffany is back to wincing.

She turns back to join her friend and says, "That's why I'm on a crusade. To rid the world of sex addicts so they won't go through what I'm going through. Surfing the Internet and dropping propaganda to anyone that'll listen. It may not work, but it makes me feel like I'm doing the right thing."

Her friend, she says, "How do you get it in your throat? Don't you use condoms?" And you can imagine the look on Tiffany's face, disappointment and disgust, knowing that her mouth has scraped dozens of knobs and tasted loads of come.

The ghosts, the voices, one says, "Fruit so it tastes sweeter? And bananas and pears?" Not once do the voices mention anything about throat clap. But liking frozen bananas and caramel apples, those are good.

"I hate the taste of rubbers," Tiffany says. She says, "But try going a day without having to build saliva because your throat is dry." She clears her throat and with every swallow, Tiffany tastes the men she's had during her life as a swinger. She swallows again and it's swinger one's juices. Then it's swinger two's juices. "Then, well," Tiffany says, "it just isn't worth it."

"Apparently, trendy and hip equate to Chlamydia of the throat," Unknown says through the pipes. He says, "That's not something you read in People magazine."

One prisoner flushes the toilet and for a brief moment, the words come out gurgled.

Tiffany says to her friend, "My husband won't even touch me anymore."

Tiffany, now a Christian, she goes to church every Sunday and prays every night, in between her continual searches on the Internet, telling anyone and everyone that she's concerned. And her husband, he's now banging his secretary at work in his office, telling his wife he has to "work" late.

To the diners in the restaurant, Tiffany, she's a non-smoker. One woman, blowing smoke out of the side of her mouth, says to her friend, "She's probably in perfect health too. Look at her skin, it's flawless."

The smoker's friend, she raises her coffee mug to her mouth, sips the drink and looks toward Tiffany's direction above the rim of the cup. She nods in approval as her friend blows out a ring of smoke.

Tiffany, being judged by those around her, she swallows again, this time hard - swinger three's juices.

Tiffany's friend, she says, "Does his secretary know?" And you can imagine the look on Tiffany's husband's secretary's face as she goes down on him while he's sitting back on his chair and his head is leaned over the headrest of his executive styled leather seat. All this, and there's an unopened condom hiding in the back of his wallet's dollar bills. The rubber has been packed in his wallet for so long the wallet's leather has a ring shape on it. The rubber's lubrication is dried out and flaky. The expiration date, it's now past due and the lettering is faded.

"Thank goodness she has a health plan, because a day's worth of swallowing, well," Tiffany says, "no one should go through that." She swallows and a little saliva fills her mouth - swinger number four.

The woman smoking, she's now putting out her cigarette and saying to her friend, "Non-smokers, they're lucky." Her friend, sipping on her coffee nods her head in agreement.

Tiffany, a beautiful woman on the outside, when she smiles, she looks like she should be on the cover of a magazine.

The suits, they see her rock for a ring, and imagine what it's like to be buried inside her. One suit, he says, "Her husband is a lucky guy. What I would give to get head from her." Then he downs his beer, swallowing harder and harder as the liquid goes down his throat. The swallowing echoes in Tiffany's brain. She closes her eyes and winces. "I'd jizz in her mouth," he says, slamming the glass to the table.

But in reality, Tiffany's throat, it has seen better days.

Tiffany says, Iugulan Neisseria Gonorrhea.

Tiffany says, It's a venereal disease.

Tiffany says, Only it breaks out in your throat.

Men that hit on her, they word their phrases, trying to get a hint about her relationship with her husband. Not good? Working it out? Something like that.

Throat clap? That doesn't cross a person's mind. One man, he says, "I guess you never know a person's story until you hear it for yourself."

Tiffany, she says to her friend, "I completely have a different look on life. Being a swinger, it made me realize that there's more to life than screwing and sucking off married men."

"But," her friend says, "it's so trendy. Having an affair, everyone is doing it." The two women, they sip the rest of their drinks and ask the waiter to bring the checks. The waiter, a baby faced college student, he smiles and eye flirts with Tiffany, and says he'll be back in a moment.

When the waiter returns, he places the checks on the edge of the table, and on Tiffany's, there's a name and a phone number. He says, in a whisper, "Call me." Like the men that Tiffany comes across, he, too, takes a stab at her, believing that her lips around his penis are something worth losing his job over.

Her lips, they are something worth losing his girlfriend over. But throat clap? That is not something ever considered.

Tiffany grabs her check, scans the total and sees the number. She shows it to her friend and says, "This guy has no clue. None whatsoever."

The table of suits, they have no clue. The woman smoking, she has no clue. But this waiter, he wants her to call him.

Tiffany, she grabs a pen from her purse, writes on a napkin, "Iugulan Neisseria Gonorrhea. It's a venereal disease. Only it breaks out in your throat." Then she takes out some money and leaves it by the napkin.

8.

"People like to make judgments about a person upon first sight. From what they're wearing, to what kind of shoes a man has on."

Stud says, "The two things that women look at first when a man enters are their face and their shoes." Stud, he's ready to tell his story.

Herpes, that's something you can't see right away. Pedophile, that's something you can't see right away. Murderer, that's something you can't see right away. Put a pair of nice shoes on, comb your hair, and chances are, you're making a good impression on a woman.

Stud, he says into the pipes, "Imagine finally getting the girl of your dreams. Imagine thinking the entire time that she's perfect. That she's everything you've always wanted. She's a non-smoker, casual drinker, she's smart, and her ex-boyfriends aren't crazy."

Stud, every time he sits across from her, he's thinking how lucky he is. The conversation is perfect, the words she chooses to say are perfect, the atmosphere is perfect, everything is perfect. It can't get any better than this. This is what Stud thinks when he's with her. When he's sipping his glass of wine, he says to himself, "This girl is perfect."

Her hair, it falls tightly down the sides of her cheeks. Her almond shaped eyes stare at Stud while the perfect words exit her perfect lips. Stud, he loves these lips. And her skin, a smooth feel, like satiny gardenia petals under his fingertips. Stud, he says, "All this, and she's a doctor. A mother bleeping doctor."

"Now," Stud says, "imagine, for one second, that she's not nearly as perfect as once thought. And your wine doesn't taste as fine as it once did. And the food, hell, the food hasn't even arrived yet. But you think that it can't be as tasteful as it did the minute you set foot in the restaurant. The atmosphere, it's now tainted, spoiling everything around it."

One voice says, "She's a dude!"

Another voice, through the pipes, it says, "She's got a dick!"

She tells Stud that she has a disease. Her expression is serious. She's planned this talk many times before. In the mirror before the date, she was rehearsing it to death in her mind, over and over, just to get it to come out right.

No matter how many times a person rehearses these words, they'll never sound right.

"Imagine, that you have a decision to make. One that will make you look like a bleeping schmuck or a godsend," Stud says. He says, "You pick. It's your decision."

She looks Stud up and down, knowing that he has a decision to make. Stud, he says to himself, "Do I stay or do I go? That's the decision."

The disease she has is a sexually transmitted one. It's a sexually transmitted one she got while having a summer fling a few years back. Does she regret it? Hell yes she does. But the nostalgia of that particular summer ranks in her memory as one of the best summers. Of course, save for contracting the bleeping disease. Actually, fucking disease. It's more serious than sugar coating it for anyone. Especially this date that she's been dodging for months. It's not that she didn't want to go out with Stud. It's just that she doesn't want to put him in this situation.

Stud says, to anyone that is listening, "Imagine this is happening to you."

This woman, this diseased woman, sitting across from Stud, is one of the most respected professionals in her office. She's a confident woman. She's great with patients, especially to the kids that come to see her solely for her lollipop selection on the receptionist's desk. The massive selection, tens of flavors and always in stock, it helps calm the children when they have to get X-rays, shots or checkups.

But tonight, at this exact moment, she's vulnerable. It's as if she is the patient clamming up so she doesn't have to disclose her mistake. She's looking for the lollipop flavor "make it feel better" and it's not readily in sight.

Right now, it's not even so much the disease that is embarrassing; rather it's the way people will look at her.

Stud, he says, "Imagine the decision you have to make knowing that you've spent months trying to get this woman to go out with you."

She tells Stud that the guy claims that he never knew he had the disease. "He had to have known," she says. The look on her face, that quizzical one, the one that says that on one night, this woman made a poor choice. The good grades, the not staying out too late, the staying away from drugs, medical school, exams, licensing, respect, all this superseded by a poor choice. A choice that makes Stud decide what to do - stay or go.

She tells Stud she was a straight "A" student. For the most part at least. Dean's List, President's List, then Dean's List again. She says, "My mother cried when I told her." Her mother, weeping like a child at the news of her only daughter being diseased. And all her father could do is shake his head.

"Imagine. Stay or go?" Stud says. He says, "This is what you're thinking."

The disease she has, it's one with no cure. One that she must explain to every man she wishes to pursue a relationship with from now on.

Stud, though, he pursued her until she caved. According to the doctor, he must really be into her if he keeps asking her out. She says, "At one point, you convinced me that I was normal; you were just so determined in being with me. I actually became excited to be out there again."

She hasn't dated in a while because having this discussion, in her mind, was too difficult. But she rehearsed, and Stud is the first person. She rehearsed the discussion every day, changing words around, making certain that it was exactly how she wanted it to hear. Playing dialog out until the exchanges went to a dead end. And now she's doing it for real.

Stud says, as a couple prisoners go off and talk between themselves, "Imagine that she tells you that she hasn't had an outbreak in over a year and that she currently is not on medication." He says, "Imagine, if you will, that even though she may never have another outbreak again, that the fucking disease will always be there because there is no fucking cure."

This woman, she says, "He had to have known."

Then, Stud says, "Imagine that the disease is the 'H' word."

Herpes.

A viral disease that causes eruptions of the skin or mucous membrane. This is what the dictionary defines it as.

Stud says, "Imagine that she tells you that all she wants to do is be honest with you. She may be a doctor, but she is a doctor with herpes. "Dr. Herpes, your next patient is in."

She says, "I always feared it would be like that game of telephone. I tell someone I have herpes, the guy I tell it to says I have chlamydia, that person says I have AIDS, and the next thing I know I'm dead." She says, "I figure not dating was a helluva lot better choice."

Herpes.

She says, "I can't even say the word."

Herpes.

She refers to it as the "H" word. A disease that made her mother cry. And made her father shake his head.

Herpes.

This is what plays in Stud's head. "Herpes, herpes, herpes. She refers to it as the 'H' word. "

This woman played the dialog in her head over and over, until she got it right. The dialog, it went from beating around the bush to take no prisoners. Stud, he laughs every time he refers to contracting herpes as beating around the bush. He says, "I beat around the bush and I got herpes. I should have just beat around my hand."

The food, it arrives and the waiter, completely oblivious of the conversation, asks how everything looks. He tells Stud to enjoy his dinner and if he needs anything, to not hesitate to ask. His name is Jim by the way.

Stud, he says, "Imagine that, for just one second that you have a full course meal in front of you and all that's going through your mind is if you should stay or go.

Oh, and that your waiter's name is Jim, just in case you need anything. Anything at all." Stud is on both knees, his head into the bowl and his hands are propped up on the sides of the bowl's rim.

Refills? Ask Jim.

"Where's the bathroom?" Jim knows where. He points at the other end of the restaurant. He says, "Just off to the side of the counter in the men's restroom is a hand sanitizer, in case you're one of those germophobes."

The plates of hot food, Stud has the prime rib by the way, sit peppered on the table with Stud's in front of him and her plates, she ordered the grilled shrimp, in front of her. Her dish, eight shrimps skewered, comes with a few sides. She gets vegetables and a baked potato. The baked potato is plain, just how she likes it. A plain baked potato with a side of herpes. This is what goes through Stud's mind as he picks at his prime rib.

The rib, it's not so prime anymore. It looks as if there is a bloody sore underneath ready to break out into little red bumps that force you to send it back and go with the fail safe – chicken tenders.

The blonde in Stud's building, she's the chicken tenders to the herpes' prime rib in this wonderful story.

"Imagine, the bottom of your plate is a bloody purple and with every piercing of your fork, more blood gushes out from underneath," Stud says. He says, "The juice spills under your mashed potatoes and gravy, giving it a purplish hue that you scoop up with your spoon. You do this to buy more time. More time to decide - stay or go."

Stud, he says, "Imagine this sight while the woman you've spent months trying to go out with is sitting across from you, waiting for you to say something, anything."

This disease she has, only a few people know about. Six people exactly - her parents, her son, her best friend, her doctor, and now Stud.

Out of every person in the world, only six people know her deepest secret, and Stud is one of them. He says, "Imagine that for just one second."

She says, "You probably regret asking me out." This woman, this diseased woman, she tells Stud that he probably regrets asking her out. She is giving him every opportunity to run the other way but Stud sits there, jabbing at his prime rib. A piece of meat that actually does taste good despite what he thought earlier.

A piece of meat that tastes better than the chicken tenders but heightens the probability you'll be on the shitter in an hour. But thank goodness, there is hand sanitizer on the counter by the faucet.

This woman, she wants an answer.

Stud, he says, "Now, imagine, you're about to say something, and Jim arrives to ask if you need any refills. Bleeping refills. Then if you need more napkins. And if there is anything else he can get you."

It has now been 25 minutes since she told Stud. And he has yet to make a decision. "Imagine that for one second, will you?" Stud says. He says, "What do you do?"

One ghostly voice says, "Forget the herpes, what about her dick?" And then there is laughter and a flush.

He tells her that he appreciates her being honest with him. How he's been wanting to go out with her for months. How Stud first saw her in the front office of the apartment complex they both live in.

Stud also notices the chicken tenders but he says, "I can have that anytime."

Stud says, about the first time he laid eyes on her, "You were wearing a red blouse with the top two buttons unfastened and a pair of western styled jeans that fit tightly around your legs until they opened up into bell bottoms." Never in Stud's dreams had he ever imagined that this woman would have herpes. Boyfriend? Husband? Kids? Sure. But not a fucking disease.

This is what Stud is telling her.

She says she understands if he wants to leave. "I don't blame you," she says. Her face, it's on the verge of sadness. Her eyes, they're closing slowly for effect. Her body sinks down until it sulks in her seat. It's as if someone pulls out the tab of an inflatable toy and it just keeps deflating before your very eyes.

She knows what Stud is going to say. The couple at the table next to them, the wife is leaning with one ear open, listening to every word being said. The husband, he's pretending to enjoy his salmon. They know what Stud is going to say. Hell, Jim even knows what Stud is going to say. This is why he keeps coming back to the table. Everyone knows what Stud is going to say except for Stud. This is what goes through Stud's mind.

Stud, through the drains, says, "Imagine that. Being the last person to know what's going on." He pauses to hear a reaction but the prisoners are all ears, save for the two talking between themselves.

One inmate says, "Shut up, I'm trying to listen here." The voices stop, and Stud, he continues with his story.

"It's OK," he says to her. "It's OK that you have a disease." Stud, he says this. But it's not OK though. What's OK is that Stud accepts it.

"You're a godsend," she thinks. This is what she's thinking. It's apparent from her smile. The couple next to them has now ordered dessert. They weren't listening after all. And Jim, now nowhere to be seen, never knew either.

All of the paranoia is in Stud's head. The thinking, over thinking and back again, it's how Stud copes with situations.

"Imagine the 'H' word never coming up while you're with this woman,' Stud says. He says this into the drainpipes. "Ever. Any question you had can never be brought up."

Then Stud says, "Imagine this, for just one second. No matter how badly you want to ask it, you can't do it."

Stud says to her, "I don't want you to have to think about it." He tells her this so she won't have to think about it when really Stud is the one who doesn't want to hear about it.

Stud, he leans into the newly bailed toilet bowl, looks deep into the bottom, and says, "Imagine the first night having sex with her. She's hesitant. Hasn't been with a man since she found out she had the disease."

Sitting on the bed, her back is to Stud because she can't bear to look. She then begins to cry. She tells Stud that every time the two of them are together she runs the risk of passing it to him. She says this as Stud imagines her riding him, reverse cowgirl, her hips rocking back and forth, trying to get Stud to come.

"Passing it to you," Stud says, as a prisoner in a different cell block flushes his toilet. Like she's Peyton fucking Manning or something. It's fourth and one and she's wondering if she should pass or run.

Stud, he's sitting there, naked, waiting to have sex with her. His penis is hard and there's an unused condom wrapped around it. All this while her back is toward him. Her hair is falling down past her shoulder blades, dying down at the middle of her back. The small of her back and the top of her crack are staring Stud in the face.

This is what's happening while she's crying and telling Stud that she shouldn't have let it get this far. She's shaking now.

This is what Stud is going through. His penis, it's now losing its hardness.

Stud says, "Imagine, finally talking her down and getting to a point where the two of you are having sex. After a couple heated exchanges and some well needed thrusting, she's asking if she can take off your condom."
A voice in the drainpipes, it interjects with, "Yeah!"

Stud says, "I do. Now imagine her going down on you, her head bobbing up and down, her lips wrapped tightly around your penis. All you see is a brain of hair, getting closer to you like it's three dimensional. A couple more bobs and she slides you back inside her."

And once again, the voice, it says, "Yeah!"

Stud's condom, it's lying on the floor in front of the bed. The two are going at it. No condom. Nothing. Just skin on skin.

"Can I come inside you?" Stud says to her. This is what Stud is thinking the whole time. Can he come inside her? The disease, it never crosses his mind. Unloading a wad of population paste, can he do that? This is what he's thinking. "Sex," Stud says, "it makes you stupid sometimes."

She says, "I want to feel you inside me but you have to pull out." This is what she tells Stud. And so Stud, he keeps thrusting until he pulls out and shoots a load on top of her chest.

Stud, he says to the other inmates, "My mouth is dried up and I'm laying there, breathing like I placed first in the Boston Marathon. The air smells like sex and there's sweat, lots of sweat, on our foreheads, our necks and our chests. All that's heard in the room are deep breaths, inhale, then exhale, then inhale, then exhale."

The two, they have sex four more times that night. The entire time Stud's condom is laying on the floor. And all four times her stomach, chest and belly button feel a shot of warm liquid every time he shoots.

She tells Stud that she's going to get on birth control. She says, "So then you won't have to use condoms." She says this, after the first night Stud has sex with her. "But if you still want to use condoms, I'll understand," she says.

She says this while the condom is laying on the floor.

Stud, he says, "Imagine having sex with her a total of 12 times, using a condom only once."

A tear falls from his eye, remembering the night like it just happened. He says into the toilet, "Imagine that, after three months to the day you first find out about her disease, the two of you break up. It didn't work out. You go your way, she goes her way."

Three months it takes to go out with her, three months he actually does go out with her, and all that's left are memories of a failed relationship.

"Now, imagine you having to explain to every woman you go out with that you have a disease. A bleeping disease. No, make that a fucking disease," Stud says. He says, "You're not sugar coating it for anybody."

Stud, a symbolic name for STD. "Because you," Unknown says, "have an STD." Stud, he says his body doesn't even feel like his own. It's like his body belongs to someone, or something else.

One ghost says, "You were better off having sex with your dog." And then the voice laughs.

"That doesn't even make sense," Unknown says, through the pipes, his head yelling down into the toilet. "But since you mentioned it."

A voice, the direction it's coming from is hard to determine through the drains, says, "Man, herpes, that sucks."

Unknown says, "One time Ambiguous and I are walking down the street and we see a dog licking itself. Ambiguous says, 'I wish I could do that.'"

A couple flushes are heard, muffling some of the laughter that is building up from the joke. Unknown, he says, "I'm sure if you ask the dog nicely, he'll let you do that."

And then laughter.

And then, "Herpes, man, that sucks."

And then a flush.

9.

When you gain something, it means that someone has lost something. Unless of course that person has taken millions of dollars, then it's that person who has lost something - freedom. There's a saying that says, "Every person has a price." And that price is a prison sentence.

Filter, he's in prison for changing computer data, data that ultimately gave him millions of dollars in his checking account. The bank noticed something strange when, for months, Filter hardly maintained a balance of a few hundred dollars.

The bank manager, he knew Filter, whose real name is unknown and was given this symbolic name. He knew that Filter was working at a retail store late at night stocking shelves with merchandise that came off the trucks. He says, "This guy only makes minimum wage." But his eyes scan the account and see a one date increase of a million dollars. Then two million, then three million, all within a week's time period.

The manager, each day, he checks the newspapers for lottery winners. He reads to see if there is a story about an inheritance or estate being passed down, anything that will give him a hint of what is happening.

Filter, he goes in and withdraws thousands of dollars in big bills, and the bank manager is saying this doesn't look right. Filter drums up conversation with the tellers, his new best friends. They smile, acting as if he everything is normal.

The tellers are instructed to carry on as usual. Their weekly meeting, usually filled with birthdays and upcoming events, is the first time every employee expresses interest.

A customer filtering money from their bank? That doesn't happen all the time. But Filter, happier than pigs in shit, collects the money without showing any signs of nervousness.

The manager, he phones the authorities, a series of investigations, and wham, Filter is in prison for filtering money.

And now Filter, he's asking Unknown, "Have you ever taken something that wasn't yours?"

The ghosts in the drainpipes, they're saying how money makes people crazy. A voice says, "The one thing I know is money doesn't always make you happy."

The ghosts in the drainpipes, they're saying how not knowing makes people crazy. A voice says, "Whenever there's a parent whose child is missing, all she wants to know is if her baby is dead or alive. It's all about closure."

Prisoners, bent over the bowls as if they're puking, they're actually yelling about the errors they've made. Their emotions go from wanting to be noticed to wanting to be important to wanting to feel sorry. For the victims they've hurt and for themselves.

You know what else makes a person crazy? Getting duped.

When you gain something, it means that someone has lost something. How about when that someone who lost something is you?

Doesn't it seem like the only things that are on the Internet are items that force people to show their true selves? You don't like sex? Then, don't click on these free web cam links. Don't click on these penis enlargement pills. Don't click on these friend finder sites. You don't like making money? Then don't click on these home based businesses. Don't click on these Nigerian schemes. Don't click on these MLM links. You don't like being charitable? Then don't click on these hurricane relief links. Don't buy these yellow bracelets. Don't pay attention to the Red Cross logo. The Internet, it just seems like it gets people to show their true selves. Think about it, there's no one around to see you so you must be doing it for yourself. Right?

No one's going to know you donated money; you do that for your own satisfaction. And certainly, no one's going to know you gave money to some man posing as a woman trying to get breast implants. Fuck it, you're anonymous.

Sol, a symbolic name because he solicited money from strangers to pay for a boob job that didn't exist.

Sol was broke and he owed his landlord rent for the last three months. He says, "I'll get a payment to you next week."

The landlord, fed up with Sol's efforts, or lack of, says, "I want the full amount or you're out." At first, the landlord felt sorry for Sol, thinking that he was down on his luck and couldn't catch a break.

He says to Sol, "Just help me out. I'm trying to be reasonable here." This was the first exchange when rent began to slip later and later each month. Sol did his best to earn money, but eventually, could not keep up.

The landlord, his tune changed from being reasonable to being cynical, thinking that now Sol is just trying to get a free meal. Sol is the Internet money scheme to the landlord. Click here if you have a heart and if you could donate a month's worth or rent. Or two months. Or three months.

Sol's job was outsourced to another country and now he's in a bind. And so Sol schemes up a plan to raise quick money. He says, "I need about a grand."

His plan, one thought of by a series of emails he received, involves a before picture, a torso shot, the front and side. His body is in a halter top and Sol's saying that he's a she and that she needs a boob job for self-esteem issues.

Thankfully for Sol, his body is skinny, a bony build, like a marathon runner and if you could, please donate to the cause. His chest's little hairs seen since childhood, the chest pubes were no match for his razor.

The ghosts in the drainpipes, one is saying how a friend tried killing herself because she put her house up for collateral to help a woman in a third world country get out of harm's way. He says, "She honestly thought this woman needed help. She sent her thousands of dollars."

The other voice says, "But she really didn't need help, did she?"

And the voice, the original ghost, says, "No, come to find out she was arrested a few months later for buying expensive cars. My friend never saw her money again."

For Sol, the first couple days, donations are in the hundreds, then the thousands, to a point where Sol cashes the money and pays his rent. Sol lotions himself up, giving the perception of a time progression, and uploads new photos. More money comes in, all because men are hoping to see this poor girl's self-esteem get boosted. Lonely men plus hopeless girl plus too much time, it's an equation that will break you.

Within a month, people are emailing him to see the after pictures. Sol says, "The doctor fucked up and now I need to get them redone by someone else."

"The cost," he says, "is an extra seven thousand dollars." His torso, bandaged up like he's a mummy, there are ketchup stains underneath fading through to the outside bandage strips.

One emailer, he's sending messages everyday asking, "What happened?" and saying, "That sucks." Then he says, "What do you look like? Talk to you later."

And Sol, his loyal following of horny, lonely men wanting to help out, asks for more money until he reaches his amount and pulls the scam another six times on different sites. Lonely, horny men, their neighbors are saying to themselves, "They're so quiet. They're so nice. Wouldn't harm a fly."

People, they scour the net to donate money for their own satisfaction. Who is going to ever know they did something like this?

Sol says, "The second time I raised the money in three days."

The way Sol matters now is because men, gullible stupid men, they become more skeptical with things.

And now society enforces stricter rules for Internet scams like these. Unknown, he says, "They're now punishable under the law with a sentence as high as so many years in prison. As if the scammers care about getting caught."

Unknown, he's in prison for feeling irrelevant. He always wants to feel important, and being in prison, talking to the other inmates, he feels like he matters.

Unknown says, "Letting people hang on to dreams, it's what people live for. Why on earth would you be alive if there wasn't hope? For anything."

There's a PSA that runs on television that ends with a caption that reads, "As long as there's hope, there's a future."

And as long as there are gullible people out there with thick wallets, there will always be scammers.

The ghosts in the pipes, through the empty bowls, they're saying how the world has become a "right now" society. "Everything is instant," one voice says. It says, "Help me out and there are millions for your assistance." Go on a reality show and you're a celebrity. Everything is so phony nowadays.

Anything can be a scam.

Right now, someone is scamming another person. According to a survey done by Internet Fraud Statistics, the ideal age group to scam is between 20 years old to 49 years of age. So what could a person sell to that age range? One man, Unknown, has that answer. And the story, it travels clearly through every drain for all the prisoners to hear.

Unknown, he got off by entertaining women with stories. Now? He's getting off with prisoners, but not in the way that you would think. He does this any time he feels irrelevant.

10.

Unknown delivers newspapers in bulk for an artsy publication. He calls himself a distributor, not to be confused with a paperboy. Everything about Unknown is better than it really is. He's never had real experience to do anything. But if you ask, he's a Distributing Specialist.
He says, "It's all in the way you present yourself."

Unknown's other job is filling out phony names on Columbia House cards. He fills out hundreds, if not thousands a year, getting free CDs, free DVDs and once they arrive, he sells them online.

Unknown, he says, "I have sometimes two or three or four of the same CD. Just put them online for a couple bucks, up the shipping and by the end of the month, I've got hundreds of dollars."

So far, he's used more than three thousand names. Names that are close to his. Same initials, names that rhyme with Unknown. Unknown as his last name. His friends' names. Names he comes up with at the spur of the moment. Ridiculous sounding names. Ones like Hugh Jass. Jenny Taylia. Seymour Butts. Anita Lay. Richard Hurtz, he goes by Dick. And Keenta Hornay.

His friend, Anonymous, is saying, "How many CDs of mine have you sold? How many DVDs of mine have you sold? How much have you made off my name?"

Before Unknown made the jump to bigger cons involving restaurants and hotels, he was perfecting his trade with smaller items.

Unknown, he says he's a Distributing Specialist. For newspapers and music.

Unknown's real name has perfect credit. Somewhere out there a Rachel McCarthy is wondering how her credit report has gotten so bad. She looks at her report once a year and now she's wondering what the judgments are against her.

The amounts, of all six judgments, they total nearly $1,200 dollars.

Brenda Nichols wants to know why she can't get a loan to buy a car. Her credit score, it's not what she imagined. "There's no way my credit score is 410," she says. She has worked hard to keep it at a respectable level but the one mistake she made was not checking her report on a regular basis.

She says, "I swore the last time I checked it was 650 or so." The Finance Manager at the car dealership, he's showing a copy of her credit report to her across the desk. Brenda eyes it up and down; it's the first time she's seen the report in a while.

The first page, middle of the page down, says that Columbia House is owed thousands of dollars. She says, "What is Columbia House?"

Chris Taylor is trying to refinance his house. His wife accuses him of spending too much on junk. The fact that in his garage is a car that hasn't seen the road for years and an old pool table has nothing to do with his bad credit. He yells back at her saying he is on the phone with his credit guru to figure out what is what.

Anonymous, he says, "What type of music do I prefer? What kind of movies do I watch? When will you stop doing this?"

Unknown says, "It's just until I get a raise or a decent paying job." With his lack of experience, Anonymous is guessing he'll be loving movies for a long time.

Anonymous says, "At least pick out movies I like."

Brenda Nichols will never get a car. If she does, she'll have ungodly high interest. But, if anything, she'll be checking her credit report more frequently. Thanks largely in part to the legend of Unknown.

Rachel McCarthy is filing bankruptcy. She's filling out the paperwork and hoping that the court lets her keep her one car to get to and from work. She's calling a credit counselor because, at first thought, she thinks she has a problem with money.

Anonymous says, "You're lucky you're my friend." Anonymous used to be like Unknown. He used to be Unknown. Thanks to Unknown, he's got hundreds, if not thousands, of CDs and DVDs. Ones Anonymous hasn't heard or seen yet.

Thanks to Unknown, his credit is screwed up. He says, "What movie did I just buy today?" One of Unknown's newspapers is on the table. Anonymous, he pulls out the ads section to see the new releases. "These movies," he says to Unknown, "they're on sale until next Thursday. Can I at least buy these ones?"

Then he turns the page and sees that T.I. has a new album out. He says, "I have never heard of this artist but I'm guessing I own at least four copies." He tosses the ads back on the table.

Unknown's job at the newspaper is an early morning one. The shift, which consists of picking up loads of bundled papers and dropping them off at various locations for distribution - coffee shops, bagel places, bookstores - takes him around three hours a day.

After, Unknown's sleeping and then selling CDs and DVDs online. His TV, it flickers its alien looking blue light, broadcasting daytime dramas and talk shows. In a given day, the television can see Oprah, Judge Judy and "Days of Our Lives."

While Unknown packs and labels products, he's yelling out questions on "Jeopardy." He says, taping down a corner, "Who is George Washington?" He scribbles the name and address that the package is being shipped to and slides it into a pile of outgoing mail.

He says, "What is muy bien?" The host on the show is saying correct, and to please select another category. Off in the corner there is a build up of packages waiting for distribution.

Unknown's online store, called Unknown's Attic, is a dot com masterpiece. It has an easy check out system, payable with any kind of credit card, he accepts money orders and also ships internationally if a higher rate is paid. His feedback is 99.8% positive with a couple neutral for taking forever to ship.

Unknown says, "Those are the ones that took forever to pay so I waited as many days to ship as it took for them to pay." He says to Anonymous, pointing with his finger, "Hand me that box right there."

Anonymous looks down and sees a shoe box filled with music, all brand new and all with Post-It notes with purchasers' names and addresses.

One goes to Nebraska.

One goes to Texas.

One goes to Puerto Rico.

All with names, addresses and a thank you from Unknown. He pulls out a movie, flips it around the back and reads the synopsis. Behind him, on the screen, a buzzer is going off. Unknown, he says, "Who is Emily Dickinson? Wait."

The host says, "Sorry, that's incorrect." Another buzzer goes off. And before the contestant speaks, Unknown says, "Who is T.S. Eliot?"

Anonymous laughs. He says, "Do you know if you re-arrange the words in T.S. Eliot's name you get toilets?"

Unknown's profit margin is infinite. Whatever he makes on selling a CD or DVD is infinite. The box of inventory begins making profit at one cent. There are tens of empty shoeboxes around the apartment. At any given time they can be valued at $1 to $500 dollars.

On the television, the host says, "This Egyptian diplomat was the sixth Secretary-General of the United Nations."

Unknown, he says, "Who is Boutros Boutros-Ghali?" None of the contestants buzz in. The host, he says, "The correct response is, who is Boutros Boutros-Ghali?" Then the show goes to commercial.

A separate sticky note on each CD and DVD has the price it sold for. Unknown logs the prices in a notebook, with the buyer's name and info so that he can pursue them later privately with music he says they may want.

Unknown says, "Kendall Tucker bought a couple Rolling Stones CDs from me. If I get a hold of any other Stones' music or concerts, I email him to let him know I have it." He says, "Same sounding bands as well. The

Wallflowers, old twangy rock bands with the gee-tar, and good ole southern rock n' roll."

"Often times, they'll ask to buy it outright so they don't have to wait for the auction," he says. "Then I throw out a price, a high one, include free shipping and I have a customer for life."

Anonymous asks Unknown his preferred method of payment. Unknown, he says, "What is PayPal? It's the way to go."

Anonymous digs through the box and together, they sort through the selection and wrap CDs and DVDs up with newspaper and brown paper bags and ready them for shipment. Unknown saves money on handling because he uses the newspapers from his other job to ship the media. "I always take out the same sections in the papers so that the customers think they were never included at all," Unknown says. He says, "They're mostly Four Season ads and car dealerships. No one ever complains."

Unknown, he spends hours in the line at the Post Office. The employees know him by name and you can guess that each postal worker has an extensive taste in music and movies. Whenever they drum up conversation with Unknown they're making it more and more difficult to buy a house.

Anywhere Unknown can get a name he's using it to purchase more inventory. An elderly woman dies and her family takes out a half-page obituary? She's now deceased with an incredible music selection. Unknown, he reads the obits daily, taking note of each person who has left the world. Unknown, he says, "By the time their families sell their estate and finish the grieving period, I would have sold a hundred movies."

"Real estate ads," he says, "are a gold mine." The realtors, always being awarded a Gold Star or Salesman of the Year, they're also nominated for Movie of the Month member. Unknown says, "They're more concerned with selling houses they don't have time to check their credit reports." When a member buys more then a dozen movies in a month, they get one free. Unknown, he says, "Then I put that free one online and it's icing on the already iced cake."

Anonymous says, "How many CDs do I own?" He waits for a response but gets nothing. Then he smiles and continues wrapping. "You're lucky you're my friend."

Then they wrap.

Personal ads looking for romance? Unknown says, "They're now committed to inheriting music. Fred, meet Marilyn Manson. You two look great together." Unknown swears he'd be a great campaign manager, saying that he could generate votes in a heartbeat. He says, "They may not all be alive or know they're voting, but still."

At the post office, Unknown tells the employees that his company is picking up and that's why he's shipping more and more frequently. They smile, thinking that he's a great entrepreneur. He says, "I also need to extend my P.O. Box for another year."

"Jeopardy" returns and Unknown says, "Shh, I wanna hear the Double Jeopardy categories." The categories flash on the screen and Unknown says, "This round will be brutal." Then he wraps another CD and slides it into the pile. He looks at the stack, watches some packages slide off the top, and then looks at Anonymous. Unknown says, "I may have to get another friend. Know anyone wanting to work for free who doesn't care about their credit?"

And Anonymous, packing and wrapping and taping, he says, "You better not be getting The Jonas Brothers in my name." Then he laughs, slides the CD or

DVD into the pile and continues. He says, "You better not be getting Jewel in my name."

Unknown, grabbing another album to wrap, says, "What is Stephen King's 'Nightmares & Dreamscapes?'" There is silence on the television screen, with none of the contestants buzzing in. Unknown, he says, "Or it could be 'Black House' by King and Peter Straub."

Anonymous makes a buzzer noise. He says, "You didn't put that in the form of a question."
On the screen, the timer goes off. The host says, "The correct answer is Stephen King's 'Nightmares & Dreamscapes.'"

Anonymous laughs and says, "You just lost all your money." He writes a name on the package and slides it into the pile. The package creates an avalanche of music and movies that force Unknown and Anonymous to stop what they're doing to restack.

One voice, through the pipes says, "It took me forever to go from cassette tapes to CDs." And then a flush is heard. And then, "Yeah, I was probably the last person on Earth to give up my tapes. I might even still have them somewhere."

11.

They say, "A picture speaks a thousand words." Well, so do fucking words. Especially when the first word that speaks a thousand words is herpes.

Stud has a story. And instantly, the voices through the drains stop. There are no flushes, no ambient TV sounds, nothing. Stud, he says, "I guess it's OK to be a murderer or a child molester, but to have herpes, well, they want no part of it. That's like a fucking disease."

A ghost in the drains says, "I heard about a high school wrestler contracting face herpes when he wrestled a kid from another school who had a breakout."

One voice says, "Really?" Then a couple voices out of nowhere, in unison, say, "Shh!"

Before Stud continues, the voice says, "Yea, they had to stop the tournament and have everyone on each team checked. Can you imagine telling your friends you got herpes from another guy you were wrestling?"

Since Stud has heard the news, he hasn't been himself. That's actually an understatement. Confused, vulnerable, afraid, a feeling that no one wants him, is more like it. This is what goes through Stud's mind, every minute, since he heard the news.

Being by people, talking to people, listening to people, as they talk about their families and their jobs, it goes in one ear and out the other because herpes is at the forefront. These people, they tell Stud about their lives because they feel sorry for him, the same way people do when they see a handicapped person.

Stud, he says, "You want to open the door for that person, you want to listen to how he placed first at Special Olympics, all because you feel sorry for him. These people, they're telling me about their lives but their lips, to me, they just move and move, with nothing coming out."

Everything is on edge, and being like this, Stud develops phobias. Different phobias that he can't explain. Phobias that have nothing to do with sexual contact. Stud says, "There are times I see fruit with mold on it and I think, 'Who did that peach sleep with?'"

The moldy beard growing on top of the peach fuzz, it's like a science experiment gone bad. "I won't even touch it," Stud says.

One time, Stud was at the grocery store and some tomatoes looked as if they ran out and became Amish. The thick row of moldy beards climbing on top of each other scared Stud to death. He jumped back a little, drawing the attention of a woman nearby holding up a cantaloupe for examination. The woman, she stopped and stared at Stud until he regained himself enough to walk away.

One voice, it says, "What about peaches? Does a peach add some sweetness?" This voice, it is still hung up on the idea that come can taste sweet.

Stud says, "Herpes. This is what I have. She refers to it as the 'H' word. The woman I got it from."

There has been no sight of her since the two broke up. Not that he was really looking. For the most part, Stud was dodging hairy produce.

For the most part, Stud was wiping off the imaginary beards that have somehow gotten on his arms.

These phobias, they now contribute to Stud's happy place, a place where he forgets intimate details of the most routine events.

This happy place, it's a means of coping with his phobias.

"Ironically, she moved from the apartment complex," Stud says. He says, "Just like that. Our relationship ends and she moves away, like she was never in my life at all. A three month relationship. That's what we had. I hate the three month gigs."

For support, a couple of voices say, "I hate 'em too," and, "Yea, me too." One voice, ghostly as if it has a long way to travel says, "My whole life is a three month gig."

And then a "right on."

And then a flush.

The ghostly voice, it says, "It's like I'm on tour with the same chick as my opening band."

A really short courtship or a really long one, this is what Stud prefers. When a relationship lasts for a couple days, it's easy to forget. There's nothing tangible about it. There are no letters, no pictures, no gifts, nothing like that. Stud, he says, "It's too soon to do shit like that. There's no trace at all. It's like a mini vacation with exceptional room service."

When the relationship lasts for years, two or three or four, there will be a batch of pictures, studio ones and candid opportunities - you and her on the beach, you and her at a party, you and her at a restaurant, one with the waiter and one without, stuff like that. Pictures, there are some with you and her with some man in the background trying to get in the shot.

According to Stud, that's how it is.

On his knees, in his cell, Stud adjusts his position to become more comfortable. The only time he ever had to lean on his toilet was when he had a hangover. Behind him, a couple prisoners are jabbing back and forth through the bars. Stud blocks them out and continues.

He says, "There are gifts, bad shirts, a tie that you never can find a shirt to match it with, maybe some pants or some tools, video games for the console she hates you playing on all the bleeping time. This is what a lengthy relationship consists of."

But with the three month ones, they're not long enough to consist of photos, bad gifts, letters that say, "No, I love you more." Nothing like that. "But they're not short enough for you to forget. Too much time has passed and you remember things," Stud says. He says, "That's what gets you. Your bleeping memory. In my case, fucking memory. I'm not sugar coating it for anybody."

Stud, adjusting his position to accommodate his now hurting knees, says, "The three month gigs, during them, the fucking facts and fictions get misconstrued. You don't remember what actually happened and what didn't. Events pop into your head and the parts you can't recall, you make them up. That's what the three month gigs represent, a bunch of facts and fictions."

The ghostly voice, it says, "The facts and fictions of a great summer tour."

And Unknown, yelling into his empty bowl, says, "And that's what makes a good story. A combination of facts and fictions." He turns his head and listens through the toilet bowl like he's trying to hear the ocean. When guards pass by each inmate's cell, it looks as if they're all synchronized, listening to the ocean via the world's largest shell.

"Sure, we fucked in a public place. I think we've done it outside. Who the hell knows? No one, so you make it up. It's the facts and fictions that get misconstrued." Stud pulls back and clears his throat.

This woman, this diseased woman that gave Stud herpes, she broke the relationship rules. It only lasted a mere three months but he will be attached to her forever. Physically with the disease, and emotionally with the phobias. Stud says, "This is what I think about when I first wake up in the morning. When the radio alarm kicks on, it's the weather, a song by an aging rock band and oh, by the way, you have herpes. And holy cow, look at that traffic. It's backed up for miles."

This woman, she bought a house somewhere across town. This is the word. A friend of a friend of an acquaintance. She put a huge chunk of money down and moved. Just like that.

She moved across town into a nice, ranch style house. It was just her and her son. His name is Freddy by the way. Freddy Herpes. Not that it makes any difference at all.

The house has huge bedrooms and an oversized basement. The basement is shaped as a 90 degree angle, enough room to put a mini-bar, pool table, big screen and home stereo system. Stud, he says, "And of course, a side of herpes. The 'H' word I mean."

The name above the mailbox in her old apartment building is now faded. The raised white letters on the thin metallic covered sticker barely make out real letters. The B looks like a P, the E looks like the letter F, and so on. The name, it reads something along the line of PIFGY something.

One time, Stud, he noticed the mail carrier trying to verify junk mail with the faded name. He said to her,

"She doesn't live here anymore." According to the mail, the advertisers were more than enthusiastic to offer such great deals to a Ms. Pifgy Herpes.

Need new tires? Then we can help you.

How about a free dessert? Then come visit us.

Your eyewear getting old? Make your appointment today.

Unknown, he says, "Don't worry, all those advertisers' credit scores are fucked up."

Stud, he said to the carrier, "Got anything in there for herpes?" The carrier, she gave Stud a look and then left the building.

The new tenant has no bleeping clue. "The person who used to live here had herpes?" That doesn't come out when the landlord shows the place.

It's more like, the woman who used to live here is a doctor. This is how it's advertised. "This doctor, she bought a nice house across town," the landlord says, "Now I need to fill this apartment. I have someone else coming in later to look at the place." He looks at his watch to give the full effect of urgency.

The new renter smiles, signs the lease and lives her life. Stud says, "Herpes free, I imagine. This is what goes through my mind every time I see her."

This woman is very pretty, very sleek. Nice legs. She plays tennis a lot. That's all Stud can tell by looking at her. She's some sort of professional. She drives a nice car, wears nice clothes, maybe a business woman or something. She tells her co-workers how she loves her new place. She says, "Oh, and it used to be rented by a doctor."

Her co-workers, they ask, "What kind of doctor?"

She shrugs and says, "Don't know. Just know that she's a doctor."

"Sometimes I just want to go out and fuck everything I see," Stud says. He says, "Spread it to those people; see how they like it."

A woman that reminds Stud of her. Her looks, personality, voice, a smile, something that triggers thoughts of this woman. Just hit on her and pass it to her. Like Peyton fucking Manning. Stud says, "It's fourth and one and I'm going for it and hoping she doesn't call an audible."

He says, "Maybe the woman who is so stuck up and 'in' to herself. You know the one? The kind that plays into the hands of every fucking guy that finds that shit attractive. I'm cute, look at me. That one. Who wants to take me home? That one. I can't believe she would walk out of the house wearing that. That one. That woman. You know the one? Plop a nice load on her chest and bam, now she's not so stuck up. The, who is going to buy me a drink because I'm so damn hot? That woman."

Unknown, listening to the story, says to himself, "Stud is my kind of guy."

A voice, it says, "Manning would be able to read the audible."

Another voice, traveling through the pipes, says, "Yea, you should change Manning to Jay Cutler."

Then there are laughs and a couple flushes.

Stud, he says, "Or the woman who asks for it by dressing like a tramp. The mediocre looking woman that continuously tells people, 'I don't know why I keep getting hit on. It's not like I'm asking them to talk to me.' But the looseness and the apparent skin makes guys' dicks wake up. Breasts plus alcohol is an equation for date rape.

Whenever Stud gets this way, he sits in his living room with the light off. There's no TV, no noise, nothing. Stud says, "It's just myself assessing, assessing my life. My brain goes into overdrive and the thoughts go racing from the moment I first saw her to the day I found out I had herpes."

There's a poster with a hot woman in a bikini that reads, "Somewhere, some man is sick of her shit." This is true, to some extent.

Stud, he says, "You never know what baggage a person brings. In the case of the 'H' word, who would ever imagine? Husband, boyfriend, kids, sure. But not herpes. Not this woman, this doctor, this mentally gifted woman. Diseases are for drug users and homeless people." This goes through his head when he is sitting alone, cross legged in the middle of the living room. STDs are for hookers and pimps. Sluts, whores, those types of people. But not a fucking doctor.

STDs are for poor people.

STDs are for stupid people.

STDs are for any other person but Stud. He says, "Even though I'm a sex addict, STDs aren't for me."

Right now, some poor sap is trying to hit on her, this diseased doctor, and when she finally agrees to go out with him, look out. "I have something to tell you." This is what she says to him.

It's nothing major, he thinks. Kids? Something like that.

"I love kids," he tells her. He says he has three nephews. That he gets along with them very well. Brownie points, this is what he sees. In his mind, he's thinking, "I'm in like Flynn." This is what goes through his mind as he gets tanked on cheap beer. "Another one," he calls out, confidence brimming.

"It's on like Donkey Kong." He says, "My nephew and I play basketball all the time."

This doctor, she's about to strike again. Her face, it's starting to get warm and her eyes are beginning to water. She sniffles, trying not to lose it.

Her date, he says, "One time I took him to the zoo. He was –"

"I have a disease," she says, interrupting.

Stud yells down the pipes, "A bleeping disease. Make that a fucking disease. She's not sugar coating it for anybody."

A voice, out of nowhere, says, "She refers to it as the 'H' word." Then there is a flush.

"What, what kind of disease?" he says. Hearing this, he thinks of all his relatives that have died of cancer, or have diabetes, or have –

"I have herpes," she says.

The man's body goes from poised to punctured. "Herpes?" he says. Now his confidence is shot. And it's also what he needs - a shot. Of something. Tequila, vodka, a shot of reality, a shot to the groins, something.

Through the pipes, echoing up each toilet bowl, a ghost says, "Throw it deep Peyton." Then it laughs.

Stud says, "Now, her date has to make a decision. He either stays or goes. This is the decision. Forget napkins, where the bathroom is, all that fucking jazz. Does he want to go out with her even though she has herpes?" His bar tab is approaching twenty bucks. Make it $25, he needs a shot.

"Somewhere, some man is sick of her shit," Stud says. He says, "That man is me. But thankfully, there is now a new man in the running."

Stud blames himself. That's all he does, every day for at least an hour, sometimes longer, sitting cross legged in the middle of his living room. He says, "I hate everyone.

I hate everything. Mostly, though, I hate myself. For at least one fucking hour, that's all I do."

Hate.

Hate, hate, hate.

Bitch.

Bitch, bitch, bitch.

Stud, he says, "Often I feel like unscrewing the light bulb, the one in my living room lamp, breaking it against the end table and using the sharp half to slit my wrists. Everything becomes a weapon to me. Forget knives, razors, things like that. They're broken light bulbs and my belt to hang myself."

He says, "Scissors through my throat."

He says, "It's my radio accidentally falling into the bathtub while I'm showering.

Stud, he says, "It's forgetting to turn off the oven when I go to sleep." These suicidal thoughts and this behavior, they are a coping mechanism to go along with his phobias. A main course of herpes with the side of slit wrists. So long as the wrists don't have moldy beards.

Stud sits on the toilet, spreads his legs and bends his head down in between his thighs. He's successfully utilized every position to yell into the bowl. He says, "When I become suicidal I'll sit on my balcony and stare out to the parking lot. This seems to calm me down. This morning, there was a couple unloading groceries. The two were happy, to unload bags. Bags of taco shells, ground beef, tomatoes, taco sauce, the mild kind because the husband can't handle the hot stuff, shredded cheese, things like that."

The couple had a gallon of milk. It was being held in the man's fingers as the rest of his hand carried a plastic bag. Through the bag, there was ketchup, cans of soup, and a loaf of bread. The man was now adjusting his leg because the bag kept becoming more awkward as he walked. At one point, to be cute, he began to hop to the door.

Unknown, he says, "They may have looked happy, but that's not always the case."

Stud says, his neck now getting tight, "Dog food, toy bones, probably for the couple's dog. They laugh, they smile, rub up against each other, and then he says, 'Lock the doors.' The automatic door locker on the sedan makes a funny sounding noise and then they walk to their apartment."

The man says to his wife, "Did you lock the doors?" He repeats himself so his wife can chase him to their front door. Friends of theirs, they say this couple is known for making people jealous.

Stud, he says, "Me? I have two more light bulbs I can break. Just bought a four pack, 100 watt bulbs. You don't have to share."

Stud says, "I can share my scissors with them. My tub is big enough for the both of them and my radio, my radio is old anyway."

The flashbacks of Stud's past life are told every day through the toilets. Lydia, Stud's friend, says, "Snap out of it. If you really regretted the whole thing, you wouldn't have dated her."

Lydia is one of those philosophical types. Very bright, her mind, it's always moving. Always racing. A degree in "I wanna know what's going on in your life so I can analyze it and tell you what I think." She got straight A's in the program.

She says, "You have to get over it."

Stud tells her that the suicidal behavior is how he "gets over it." "You don't get it," he says to her. "You're not the one with herpes. What baggage do you have? The outside looks great but I'm sure there's some man out there sick of your shit."

Lydia laughs, as Stud blanks out into the parking lot full of cars. She says, "I'm just saying that you need to focus on other things."

He says, "Like you?" Then, Stud stands and finds a place on his living room floor. He says, "Drug addict, cable stealer, you works as a phone sex operator. Somewhere, some man is sick of your shit."

Stud goes on and on until Lydia gets sick of it. "Milking the government out of aid, collecting child support from a man who isn't the father because he's rich, nailing your boyfriend's brother because he's better looking," Stud says. He says, "Somewhere, some man is sick of your shit."

Lydia, the voice of reason in this conversation, says, "You're too together for this bullshit." This is what Lydia says, while she sits on a lawn chair on Stud's balcony watching two young kids kicking a ball back and forth.

Stud, he's now sitting on his couch flipping through channels. Next to him is the lamp with a perfectly together light bulb, and the illumination, it's blaring under the shade.

"Look at these kids," she says, screaming back into Stud's apartment. Lydia, she wants Stud to come back out on the balcony where she's been sitting since early morning. The entire time she was sitting on the balcony, Stud went from his destructive kill himself phase to 'what the hell am I going to eat today?' And is Barbara fucking Walters still on TV?

"Those kids," she says, pointing.

Outside, there is a boy and a girl, both around the age of three, maybe a year or two years apart, kicking a multicolored ball back and forth. The ball, it looks like a rainbow on acid. It's crazy and when the ball gets kicked, the picture gives Stud a headache. When it's kicked, the picture gives Lydia a headache.

It reminds them of one of those super balls you bounce really, really high, only to have it bounce down the road. The colors on the ball, it's like this ball being kicked. And your super ball, it's bouncing down the street as the colors disorient your eyes. When that happens, now, you have to get on your bike and peddle after it but you never find it. You see it though, bouncing, the colors making you dizzy until it just disappears in the grass. And, what happens? You lose a quarter out of it and now you're asking your mother if she has change. That ball, bouncing down the street with its colors spinning, it gives you a headache. But you still ask your mother for some change, for that headache to repeat. That's what this ball the kids are playing with represents, the continual headache. Back and forth, from the boy to the girl. Just like losing it in the grass and buying another one.

Stud says, "What about them?"

"Just watch," she says, pointing to the little boy.

The boy, he kicks the ball and the girl chases it. She kicks it back to him. The process repeats, back and forth, and Stud watches this, asking what's the point? This process, the ball going to him and then to her, over and over.

Stud, he's saying to himself how under his lamp is a light bulb he can break to use on Lydia's neck. And now his memory is going back to the super ball he lost when he was a child. Stud, he says, "What about them?"

Then, the little boy kicks the ball super hard into the little girl's stomach. The girl, she wails, her lungs like a bull horn, tears pouring out like Niagara, loud, obnoxious, but Stud and Lydia continue to stare.

The girl's face turns bright red, and her forehead is now reeking of sweat. Her cry, it gets louder and louder, so her mother can tend to her. She rubs her stomach and then crouches over, crying, balling, until her mother can tend to her. The little girl slows down her cries and looks over at her house.

Once again, Stud, he says, "What? What am I looking at?"

"Just watch," Lydia says again. The two watch until the mother comes out. She screams at the boy and consoles the girl. Instantly, the little girl stops crying. Her tears, they disappear as if they never started.

The screaming from the mother makes the little boy teary. Her body language is stern, and now the boy is in a full-fledged weep session. He sniffles a few times and then wipes the tears from his cheeks with his hand.

The mother pulls the girl into the house. The boy, standing alone, stops crying, smiles and runs to the ball. Now, he's happy. He's the happiest he's been all day. The frustration on his face, it's no longer existent. There is a smile, bigger than normal. It's a sense of accomplishment and can be seen from outer space. The boy picks the ball up and tosses it up in the air. Sometimes he catches it, sometimes he doesn't. He doesn't care though. He's happy.

Stud says, "It's like finding the super ball."

The ball, when it's up in the air spinning, it gives Stud a headache. The ball, when it's up in the air spinning, it gives Lydia a headache.

"See that?" Lydia says.

Stud, he's still confused. His head is beginning to spin so he focuses his attention away from the multi-colored ball. He says, "See what?"

"That boy," Lydia says. She says, "You need to be like him. The boy has no care at all. His smile, it's bigger than it's ever been all morning, and he's tossing the ball up in the air. If he catches it, that's great. But if he misses it, well, that's great too."

Stud looks at the boy, who at this time is sitting on the grass. The ball is a few feet away from him. The boy digs his heels into the green grass, picking some of it up to expose dirt. He rubs the dirt in between his hands and fingers and then throws it out in front of him. He does this over and over and one time, the wind blows the dirt back into his face. The boy closes his eyes and licks his lips to rid the dirt. He makes a face of disgust, but picks up more grass to do it again.

Lydia, she says, "That boy knows his mother treats his sister better."

Stud says, "So?"

"So," she says. "This boy has to become stronger because girls always get treated better. Girls need more attention, more love." The two watch as the boy stands to his feet. He looks toward his house, and then to the ball.

Lydia says, "You know, girls get treated better, by society, by everyone. When a man has sex with a minor, he's a predator. But when a woman has sex with a minor, she must be fucked up in the head."

Tex, he says through the pipes, "I take offense to that."

Stud says through his toilet, "Sorry Tex."

And Tex, he says, "Forgiven. Proceed." Stud continues with his story, about Lydia, a philosophical woman.

Lydia says, "Imagine what this woman feels like. She has the disease but she's not depressed like you. She knows she'll get treated better, by society, by everyone.

You, you need to do something because nobody out there will take care of you."

The boy runs inside his house. The ball, it sits still on the grass. Every now and then the wind blows it a couple inches either way.

Lydia, she says, "She lives her life, and you need to live yours. The boy finally got his act together by kicking the ball into the girl's stomach. Now, he has the ball all to himself. He has the world in his hands so to speak. He did something."

The boy then runs out of his house and kicks the ball as hard as he can. Stud and Lydia watch as the ball leaves the ground. The ball goes into the street and rolls underneath a car.

The spinning colors give Stud a headache.

The spinning colors give Lydia a headache.

The boy then runs back into his house, grabs another toy and comes back outside. Lydia says, "He's taking control of his life and not letting his life control him. The girl, she'll just find a doll to play with or something. She'll be fine."

Tex's voice, it zips through the pipes, and says, "How old is this little girl?"

A couple prisoners say, "Hey!"

Stud stops and waits for more talking. When there is none, he continues.

Lydia, she says, "The girl's just happy because her mother fixed the situation. She's now taken care of."

And that's when it hits Stud. He says, "I'm holding on to this woman, the diseased woman, the one that gave me herpes. She's the little girl and the ball is my life. This woman, this diseased woman, she doesn't care to be associated with me. I'm kicking my multi-colored ball to her but she kicks it back. I need to take it and do something with it."

Unknown, he says through the drain, "Take your ball and go the fuck home."

"You need to get your life back," Lydia says. She says, "Just like that boy. See how happy he is?" The boy stands to retrieve the ball from under the car. He pulls it out and throws it up as far as he can, only to see it fall down   with   complete   freedom.

Lydia says, "You're only as secure as you want to be."

Stud says, "I'm only secure as I want to be."

And slowly, surely, Stud gets his life back. That light bulb, it's not needed after all. Stud, he says, "Maybe my theory on relationships is true. I hate the fucking three month gigs."

12.

"One of the easiest ways to get away with something," Unknown says, "is to talk intelligently about a topic that's hard to understand. There's research to be done, of course, but don't tell me you can be a good scam artist if the scam isn't thought out well. With every scam, there has to be a victim. In my case, it was women."

Unknown takes his position at the front of his toilet, his hands propped up on the sides and his head just above the bowl. "Tom Cruise's manager, investing in stocks, it's the same thing," Unknown says. "They both lead to the same result."

He says, "It's no different than how Steele got here. He took money, the result of robbing the bank. Steele could've gotten money by counterfeiting it or by embezzling it but he chose robbing the bank. The result is the same."

What's important is that Steele's crime, Unknown's crime, all of the prisoners' crimes serve a purpose in society. If it's to teach a woman to be more cautious about men approaching them, then so be it. If it's to get a neighborhood watch sign in the area, then that's what it is. "All of these results," Unknown says, "they make us feel important."

Unknown, sexually, physically and psychologically abused as a child, now wants everyone to feel like he did - wanted. He now wants everyone to feel like he did – used. Unknown, he's in prison for deception. He's in prison for fraud.

One of the cons he has used is saying he invests in stocks. He does this, acting like he's someone else, when he feels anxious or stressed. Unknown does this when he wants to meet women.

Unknown, he says, "I invest in stocks. That's what I do." He says this to a beautiful woman he's hitting on. This woman, she humors Unknown by engaging him. After all, Unknown looks normal. It's not like he said, "I'm not a psycho or anything."

This woman he's talking to says, "Like what?"

Unknown invests in mostly NASDAQ stocks, tech stocks that have a high return. "I have a pretty diverse portfolio," Unknown says. He says, "With a mix of mutual funds and Dow stocks."

The woman, her interest now peaked, raises her eyebrows impressed by the legend of Charles Schwab. She currently has nothing saved for retirement but here is this man, canoeing down a river of money.

He says, "Do you know that if you would have invested $1000 dollars in Amazon.com at inception, in six years you would've had five million bucks?" Unknown smiles, and says, "The CEO of Amazon, Jeff Bezos, he's worth eighteen billion dollars."

This woman, she says, "I buy books on that site all the time. I always check there first because the prices are so much better." Then she says, "Five million huh?"

Unknown nods. He says, "Here's a guy whose net worth increases a quarter of a billion dollars each year, all because he created a virtual library with unlimited book space. It also helps that he unveiled the Kindle, but still."

He leans into her and says, "But you know what the most amazing thing about Jeff Bezos is? He didn't turn a profit for seven years. That's just unheard of for a small business."

The woman, she raises her eyebrows, impressed by this information. She says, "Stocks, huh?"

Unknown, he tells her that a stock this current year had a two for one stock split. "I now own twice the amount of shares," he says. The fake shares, they add up pretty easily. A two for one split is nothing in make believe land. Unless those shares are in Columbia House.

She says, "What's that mean?"

"It means," Unknown says, "that if you own 100 shares in a stock at fifty dollars and it has a two for one stock split, the stock is now worth $25 but you now own 200 shares." He's explaining this as if he's giving a seminar to new employees, all without pie charts and fancy colors.

Unknown, he says, "When the price of a stock gets high, then the company usually has a stock split to entice shareholders to buy more, stuff like that." These lies, they roll off the tongue as if they're geared toward certain people.

This woman, her eyes are bigger than when Unknown first began speaking and now she's following as best she can. Her interest has lost it momentum the more and more confused she gets. She smiles and nods her head to play along. This grin and bear it tactic has been passed down generations. It was the same tactic Unknown used when his mother was abusing him.

Unknown, he sounds like a broker of some sort without the cheap suit and clip-on tie. A perfect door to door salesman. Someone you'd open the door to because you'd think he was a neighbor asking to borrow sugar.

This woman, she opened up the door without asking who it was.

A ghost interrupts and says, "You sure do a lot of research when lying." A couple of the guys say, "Shh!" and Unknown's continuing with his story. Behind him, inside the drains, the ghosts in the pipes, they talk about how one guy is in for armed robbery while the other guy is in for, well, it's a number of things. The voice, it says, "At least fifteen years."

This woman Unknown's talking to, she says, "I have a 401K plan." Her name is Henrietta and she's a manager at a retail store at the mall. The store, which sells an expensive line of women's clothing, is having an after work gathering at a night club. She says, "Our parent company offers one to management."

This retirement plan is offered to Henrietta and a few other people in her store. The employees are spoon fed information; they're taught how much to allocate and to which fund, high risk, medium risk and no risk. Every now and then, Henrietta is on the computer changing the percentages from each account. She says, "They tell us to mix it up and use the one hundred year rule."

The 100 year rule, it's explained by a 401K guru, a company employee whose only job is to travel, talk to employees and educate them on how to manage a retirement plan. And Henrietta, she checks once a week, once a month, and then once a year, only to see her account jump a mere percentage higher. The small amount satisfies her enough to keep working, putting more and more of her paycheck into retirement.

The table behind Henrietta is filled with women, all dressed in clothes that were once hanging on the racks at the store. A few are sipping cocktails, while others are smoking cigarettes. They're talking about nothing in particular, this and that, and how one's thinking about changing jobs.

Unknown says, "The one hundred year rule. Subtract your age from one hundred and that is the percentage of how much money you should be investing." He says, "If you're twenty five, then you should have seventy five percent invested in your future."

The women at the table, they're lighting smokes, laughing and drinking, and one is saying how she's waiting to hear back from a potential company. "Mid-management," she says, taking a puff of her cigarette. "It'll pay me about five thousand more."

Unknown noticed the table when he first walked into the club. Henrietta jumped out at him instantly. She was sitting, her body relaxed, her arms to her sides and her eyes moving from each person that was talking as she sipped her drink one gulp at a time.

Henrietta, she says, picturing the print outs her employer sends every quarter about her finances and earnings, "I don't know exactly how much is in there, but I know I have one." She says, "I never know how to read those things. These reports are supposed to be easier to read than on the computer. I just see the gain or loss and if it gains, I'm happy."

Some laughter comes from the table. Henrietta peeks to see what's going on and then refocuses on this man, this apparent door to door salesman. This man who's selling something she hasn't figured out yet.

An hour ago, Unknown was sitting at the bar of a strip club talking to a few of the girls who were making their rounds of dollar dances.

Sarah, Teresa, and Samantha, these are their real names, are discussing with him about new features they would like to see in the club. Unknown, he knows their real names because they're close, real close.

He says, "The only problem with bringing in a special feature every month, like an adult film star or famous centerfold, is the club is only topless. The features usually tour around the country going to full nude clubs."

Sarah, the flawless skinned beauty who has been dancing for a couple years, says the club should be full nude then. She's cute. Her shoulder length hair, it's straight and curls up at the bottom, like the letter J, lots of them. Her smile, it's innocent and her teeth are small, a front one being crooked.

Unknown explains how the bar has a liquor license and the city won't allow a full nude club to have a bar. It would have to be BYOB and a lot of the bartenders will have to go and that it would just be a good idea if things were kept the same. Unknown, he says to Sarah, little innocent Sarah, "Do you want to be the reason why they lose their jobs?" He gestures to Smitty, a bartender pouring a glass of draft beer for a regular.

Sarah looks, smiles and says, "Guess not." Then she looks around the empty club, waiting for a rush of college fraternity members, businessmen or the occasional bachelor's party.

Unknown, pulling out a couple singles and sliding them underneath Sarah's garter, says, "It'll pick up. Just give it a couple more hours."

Sarah, Teresa and Samantha, they're Unknown's friends. Even though they're standing next to him with no tops on, he looks them in the eyes and not the nipples. But if asked, their nipples can be described as Hershey's Kisses, Candy Corn tops, and M&M's.

When Sarah needed a place to stay, she called Unknown's apartment, home.

When Teresa needed someone to co-sign on her car loan, Unknown signed his name, his real name. Not one of the names he uses to get free entertainment.

When Samantha needed to get back at her boyfriend, Unknown had sex with her. He said, "It's my pleasure." Over and over it was his pleasure.

Of course, these grand gestures he does aren't because they're close, it's because these girls are an investment and a commodity. Both at the same time.

Talking to strippers has given Unknown confidence to talk to women he meets at clubs. He uses them for self-esteem matters just as they use him to pay rent, pay for daycare or pay for their drug habits.

These strippers benefit Unknown's personal life, both physically and psychologically. It is how he copes with life.

Unknown, he says to Henrietta, "You must get a pretty nice discount then."

Henrietta, drinking a Vodka Tonic, looks down at her clothes and says, "Yeah, that's the good thing about working retail." She wiggles her wrist and a few bracelets jangle together until they're comfortable again on her arm. She says, "These too, we have loads of jewelry. Bins of 'em."

She looks to the table of colleagues and says, "No way girl." She's in and out of their conversation, bouncing back from them to Unknown, and back again. Laughter erupts from the table.

Unknown says, "I'm sorry, I don't even know your name."

"Henrietta," she says, extending her small hand with perfectly painted finger nails. She says, "I just got my nails buffed."

"Unknown," he says. He grabs her hand, very light and soft, and shakes it. Her skin is smooth and there's a scent of coconut on it. "Your hand smells good."

She looks at it and says, "Oh, it's from Avon. It's coconut." She pulls her hand back but the smell lingers for a second before disappearing. It suspends itself in mid air, long enough to seduce Unknown's senses.

Sarah, Teresa and Samantha, their scents are cotton candy, watermelon, and peach.

Now, the introductions are complete and Unknown says, "The hours must suck though."

Henrietta agrees and tells him that she hates closing. The store closes at nine and then she has to count down the register and make sure the store is ready for the person who's opening in the morning. She says, "It's a process but I'm used to it. Putting the change in little envelopes, and then grabbing all the receipt tape, it's definitely a process." Henrietta, she's closing down the store and leaving at about ten to ten. "But," she says, "I'm used to it."

She says, "But look at me," giving Unknown this hand gesture inviting him to take a glimpse. Henrietta, all five feet of her, from head to toe is dressed sharper than the designers themselves. Underneath her clothes, Unknown guesses that she weighs approximately 98 pounds.

Her hair, the back of it, it's tightly wound in a bun. There's one single strand falling down her forehead that curves back over her ear, meeting with the rest of her hair, fallen after a long day of selling clothes. Her hair, it's streaked with a hint of blond that complements nicely the light brownish strands that fill the rest of her scalp.

Coiled in a bun Unknown can tell that her hair is about shoulder length. Coiled in a bun Unknown can tell that, once down, it would look good while she rides him to high heaven. All this with the scent of coconut. All this with bracelets, jangling around her wrist, a noise like a maraca.

Her blouse, the top two buttons undone to show just the right amount of skin and cleavage. "Rayon," she says, "Rayon is the material." Then she pats the wrinkles out.

Her pants, they have no pockets in the front, and are jet black and fit like they've just come back from the tailor's.

She says, "These were the last pair we had in stock. My boss, the general manager of the store, almost flipped when she found out I bought them."

"Because they're supposed to be for the customers?" Unknown says.

She nods and says, "I get my pants altered when I buy them. I have the butt fixed on my pants, so they lift and separate my cheeks."

She turns to show. Unknown, he says, "You've got a nice butt." He says this because he wants her to feel like he feels – wanted. He says this because he believes it. He says this because he wants to be buried penis deep in it.

Henrietta tells Unknown that she hates the teenagers that hang around the mall after school. She says, "Some of them freak me out. I don't know if they're going to steal anything or not."

Some teens, with their gothic attire, long black skirts and black boots. "Why do they come in my store?" she says. "We don't have anything for them. The Hot Topic is on the other side of the mall." She says this, catty, as if it happens on a regular basis.

"These Goth teens, they are freaks and only want attention from the world." This is what Henrietta says about them. And Unknown, he says, "Speaking of freaks, did you know that Amazon's Jeff Bezos dumps millions of dollars into a rocket that can land vertically?"

The table near them, the conversation is now about a guy who's sitting a few yards away. "Talk to him," one woman says, "he's looking over here at you." And the other woman, she's saying how she hopes to get this new job. She says, "Then I can get that new car I've been wanting."

Unknown looks at the guy at the next table. He says to himself, "Another door to door salesman."

Henrietta tells Unknown, she says that one time a group of punk rockers and Goth chicks came in and just loitered around the store. She says, "I knew they were stealing stuff so I asked them for help and then they bailed."

When Unknown notices Henrietta's drink disappearing from the glass, he buys her another one. A Vodka Tonic. Henrietta finishes the rest of the drink in her hand and her tongue moves around the straw. Her eyes peer over the rim of the glass at the table where her friends are.

Henrietta, she says, "Go talk to that guy if you like him." The guy, whose normal face, normal haircut, normal job, normal name, his background will tell you that he had been arrested for vehicular manslaughter when his 1999 Dodge Neon crossed the yellow line and hit someone head on, killing them instantly. This normal guy, his blood alcohol was far from normal at three times the limit. However, to Henrietta's friend, he's another Unknown.

Unknown, he says to the forever disappearing bartender, "A Vodka Tonic."

Henrietta smiles at the bartender and turns back to Unknown and says, "One time we had mall security there because some girl tried stealing a pair of pants. She took them to the dressing room and stuck them between her legs, hiking them up to her crotch, and tried walking out with them." Henrietta mimics the procedure, walking a couple steps with fake pants between her legs. It looks as if there is an invisible balloon in between her legs.

"The girl," Henrietta says, "she looked like a penguin when she was walking out. It was so bad." The security came and now the girl is on probation and is banned from the store. In the store's office, there is a list of names banned from the store.

Henrietta then says, "I was the one working that night and probably wouldn't have noticed her if the store wasn't so dead at the time. Too bad too, this girl looked normal."

Unknown, he has lots of theft stories he could share but, if you ask Henrietta what he does, he says, "I invest in stocks. Because stocks is a normal job for a normal guy."

This woman, Henrietta, can talk. She has a mouth on her and the way her lips move while she speaks excites Unknown.

"Somewhere, some man is sick of her shit."

Henrietta says, "I'm a single mother of two." You wouldn't be able to tell it because with these particular clothes, her body is rock solid. It's duct tape rock solid, an entire roll's worth. The kind you eventually see later on, and when you peel off the tape, you see her body jiggle.

"Right now," she says, "my kids are with my mother." Henrietta grabs her purse from the table next to them, and pulls out pictures of her children. One photo shows two kids, staring into the camera, smiling with that blue felt step and cardboard backing for scenery. Henrietta, she had copies and copies made. One child, his elbow on the step and his fist, it's propped up underneath his chin. He's looking into the camera and smiling.

Henrietta's husband left her for a younger, more vibrant woman. Henrietta says, "After we had kids, it just changed."

The desire wasn't there anymore and once she got the kids to sleep, she was too exhausted to have sex. She says, "So he cheated. And then he ultimately left."

At first, Henrietta blamed herself. But then, soon after, according to Henrietta, her girlfriend told her that it wasn't her fault, that her husband was just a dog and that she shouldn't have married him to begin with. Now, her friend is taking Henrietta out as much as she can.

Her friend, she says things like, "Now, let's go find you a nice guy. You can do better than him. I told you not to go out with him in the first place."

Unknown, he says, "Should you have?" Henrietta shrugs and Unknown buys more drinks. He says, "I don't know why he cheated on you. You're absolutely gorgeous and I'm afraid to leave you here because if I do, then I might miss out on the magic that might happen."

Unknown, he's in prison for deception.

Unknown, he's in prison for fraud.

Henrietta says, "When he left I decided to get into shape. I bought one of those Yoga tapes." Her eyes, filled with excitement, as if she did something miraculous. She says, "Have you ever tried Yoga?"

Unknown, he says, "Tried it. I don't like it as much as Pilates but it's a good exercise to do when your muscles are tight."

Henrietta, she says, "I love it. It's a great work out and is actually effective for me." She flexes her bicep and tells Unknown to feel, her bracelets jangling in the process.

"Wow," Unknown says. He says, "It seems to be working."

Henrietta says, "Lifting your own weight is much better than lifting barbells." Unknown can tell. Her body looks like Linda Hamilton in The Terminator. She says, "Lifting barbells all the time just adds mass."

She smiles and Unknown buys her another drink. And then another one. This one before she even finishes the one in her hand. Rows of half empty glasses sit in front of them, all with straws that were once played with by Henrietta's lips. This drink, it's a double and by the end of the night, Unknown is seeing what her husband left behind.

Unknown, he's investing his stock in Henrietta and is getting an amazing return. This is how he copes with his life.

13.

Tat is crazy. This is what Ambiguous says about him. "He's just a different kinda fella." A seemingly normal person at first sight, Tat came into the prisoners' lives for beating a night club owner to death with a crowbar. The sudden anger for no apparent reason goes hand in hand with Tat's life.

Tat's right arm is filled with one continuous tattoo, curving around the elbow and around his forearm. It's part dragon, part thorny ensemble and a mix of other designs. His back has an enormous eagle smack dab in the center. Its wings, they're spread across each shoulder blade and when Tat flexes, the eagle appears to be flying. The colors, some are faded and in desperate need to be touched up, and the composite, it's an art gallery of tattoos.

Tat says, "The eagle is endangered. So don't fuck with me."

Tat, the symbolic name because of his extravagant tattoos. Tat is in prison for crushing a club owner's skull for not serving one last drink when "last call" was yelled. The bartender ignored Tat's several attempts of being served, and eventually shook his head and continued to wipe down the bar.

He smiled because Tat was a semi-regular customer and he thought, well, the bartender thought that nothing would come out of the minor exchange.

"He walked out to his car, grabbed an iron and bludgeoned the bartender to death." This was the story told by several eye witnesses. And, "I can't believe something like this would happen." The club's business has dwindled since then and there have been plenty of instances where flowers appear out of nowhere. "For one last drink," people write in letters and leave at the scene.

Tat's story, his tale of why he freaked out that night, justified by no one but himself, revolves around a dream. Tat's eyes, tearing up and his body showing remorse, says, "You know if you die in your dreams, you're dead. Supposedly, this is what happens." Officials, they listen while Tat is handcuffed.

He says, "In my dream, I'm walking with my mom and we veer off into a cemetery. For no reason, I thought. My mom, she says, 'I want to show you something.' We take a few steps farther and there it is, a grave, a headstone, with my name on it."

The dirt around the grave is untouched. There are no flowers and the stone, it hasn't been brushed for months. Tat looks at the dates. They read 1975-1991. He says, "I'm sixteen years old."

In the dream, he looks at his mother, and his mother, showing no remorse, emotion or even the slightest bit of care, turns around and leaves. It's almost as if she is happy to get rid of him. This dream, so vivid in nature, bothers Tat. He wonders why his mother lacks concern for him. This blatant ignoring, it brings up past events that are clouded with details to the forefront of Tat's life.

All the times Tat made excuses for his mother, he was justifying his wanting to be loved. This traumatic revelation, it forced Tat to go out and physically change his appearance so that he had another chance of being loved by his mother.

In his dream, Tat yells for his mother, who at this point is standing on the road leading out of the cemetery. She addresses him by looking and then walks down the road toward the entrance.

Tat, his eyes now red and his cheeks, watered down like a sprinkler let loose on his skin, says, "All I could do was step on my grave. It was almost as if I was saying, 'Fuck you. I'm still here.'" Tat looks up at the officials and apologizes for his language. "But it wigged me out." He says, "That was four days before the incident. I haven't slept for four days."

The judge says, "Why were you wigged out? Because of your death, or your mother's abandonment?"

Tat stares expressionless; he has no idea of the answer.

The judge, he says, "I understand you had a bad dream, but that dream cannot transfer to real life. Your motherly issues resulted in an innocent man's death."

Unknown, through the empty bowl, says, "The result is the result of the result." He says, "Our past determines our future, and wherever in our lives we were steered away, the result are times where people suffer."

Stud, he says, "That's why they enact laws for the shit we do. It's to protect us from us." Stud, he's taking Lydia's advice. He is taking control of his life, in prison, away from others he can hurt.

Tat, he says to the judge, "Sometimes the lack of sleep does weird things to you." Tat's attorney asks if Tat's sleeping now. He says, "I'll take any dream over the reality of that guy's face. The blood, the deformity, they're ingrained in my head."

The bartender was bludgeoned to death by a person who wanted one last drink. And flowers, they're appearing by the bouquets. And letters, folded up neatly by the flowers' stems, they say things like, "You'll be missed," and "Best bartender around."

Tat agrees to a plea bargain; he'll spend the rest of his life behind bars. "But," he says, "I'm sleeping better."

Unknown says, "That's how we all got here. We reached a point in our lives where we needed justification, an answer to calm ourselves. Whatever it was, insecurity, irrelevance, or in Tat's case, a lack of sleep, our nature was to break the rules."

Nose, he says, "That's what separates us from those out there. People, they go to church, they pray, or they meditate or do Yoga, that's how they deal with their lives. That's how they deal with stress, with distractions, with pain."

The ghosts in the drainpipes, through the empty toilet bowls, one voice is saying how he once beat up a man because he looked at him wrong. "Wrong," he says, "I don't even know what that means now." The voice, it's much calmer and relaxed, more bearable. His memory of the event lacks substance. He can't even remember when it happened. Being locked up, it makes the days creep by.

The other voice says, "That's why I never look at anyone in the eyes anymore." The voice, it echoes down the pipes, for anyone to hear, to agree with, to comment on. The voice says, "Some guy, he was drunk, he says to me that I'm the only guy in the bar that can take him in a fight. He says this because he's three times bigger than me." The voice zooms down the drainpipes, and at times, the eeriness of the conversations really do sound like ghosts.

Stud says, "I know what you mean. It sucks being the little guy."

When Tat is in the cafeteria, he sits alone, scooping up his slop with his fork while his right arm is wrapped around the tray like he's protecting it. Tat's eyes never once make contact with what's on the fork. They're just staring across to whoever is close to him.

Thanks to Tat, patrons are monitored more closely. If they're too drunk, then they have to leave the bar. The new bartender, he's only heard stories of what happened. And you can bet that whenever someone asks for a drink, he's more careful of what to say and how to react toward him. Like the other employees, he looks at the place where Tat left his freedom, organized by flowers and letters.

"Have you ever been fooled by a man, though?" Jack says, silent until now. His voice is shaky, as it echoes down paths and paths of pipes acting as telephones. He's been waiting to talk about his experience with a transvestite he met at a burlesque show. Jack, he says, "Kelly was the most beautiful woman I'd ever seen. That was until I took her back to my place and found out she had a dick." He says this with a straight face, and the prisoners, they're saying to themselves, "What the fuck?"

"A dick," Jack says, "a dick like a submarine." He says, "Filled with semen." And then he laughs, laughs so he can rid the mental image of the transvestite's huge man dick. "She sure fooled the hell out of me."

Jack sits in front of his toilet, yelling down into the bowl like it's a well with a small child trapped inside. He's in prison for murdering a transvestite. Jack jabbed a pencil in his ear and twisted until it was lodged halfway into his brain. Right there, in his room, the transvestite, Kelly, sat, screaming, as his eyes bulged and blood squirted from his head. His panties, wrapped around his ankles and his penis, it was limp and hanging between his legs.

Jack says, "I would do it again if I had to," as mental images of an uncircumcised penis enter his head, with a bush of pubes around it and little leg hair on his inner thighs.

Kelly said to Jack upon discovery, "Sometimes I shave my pubes so my penis looks bigger. It gives me an inch or so more." Jack's expression went from excited to betrayed. His emotions, the embarrassment, they ran amok through Jack's body. Then Kelly, she said, "I thought you knew I wasn't a woman." And then Jack, in one instance, he was screwing in the pencil until Kelly bled to death.

Jack was caught miles away with a semi-chubby and his underwear partially stained from premature ejaculation. The gay bar where he picked Kelly up in now has hired security.

"Like Tat," Unknown says, "Jack is making it more fun and safe for people to go out. No one should have worries like that when they party."

In the drainpipes, the ghosts talk about how one man landed in prison because of a Halloween prank. The voice, it says, "One season I handed out ice cubes to the kids. Just put them in a punch bowl and cup the cubes in your hand and place them in the bags. Put enough of them in there. With the weight of the candy and the wetness of the ice and bottom of the bag, the candy ends up falling out of the bottom." The other ghost laughs, an echo through the pipes.

And Ambiguous, he's saying how he misses his child.

The ghosts in the pipes, one voice is saying, "But what landed me here was the next season."

The other voice, in his echo, he says, "What's worse than seeing kids crying about having no candy?"

The ghost, the one with the Halloween pranks, he says, "Kids are much better off weeping and crying over no candy than biting into a candy bar with a razor blade in it."

And Ambiguous, he's remembering how his wife was caught banging another man, memories of his body in between his wife's, and her legs wrapped around her lover's waist. This looped visual, like a broken film reel, tortures Ambiguous daily. His mood swings change on a regular basis.

The ghost, feeding razor blades to children, says, "I guess that wasn't so funny after all."

14.

There are fourteen steps that determine if you're sexually compulsive. Just one and you're screwed - literally. Just one and people begin to look at you as a pervert, as someone who has "problems." You're looked at as someone whose childhood was so fucked up it drove you to addiction.

"Let's go out to this place," Unknown says to Stud. Unknown likes to throw others in the stories for effect. "This," Unknown says, "makes it believable." But when Stud uses Unknown, or Ambiguous, in a herpes story, well, they want nothing to do with it. So what does Stud do? He uses Unknown anyway.

Stud, yelling through the drains, says to Unknown, "You like to have sex with women, right?" And Unknown, he's now wishing that his stories were about murder. He smiles, and grants Stud his blessing to violate him in any way.

Ever since herpes became Stud's new best friend, his friends have tried to cheer him up. No one more so than Unknown. Unknown is a sex addict who believes it's more important to get laid than anything.

"The 14 Steps," Stud says, "are courtesy of Sexual Compulsives Anonymous International Service Organization."

Unknown, he says through the pipes, "There's that word again, anonymous."

Step number 7) Sex was compartmentalized instead of integrated into our lives as a healthy element.

"124," Unknown says. This is how many women he's slept with. This is what he says but Stud is pretty sure the number is right. He can mentally count them out in his head but that would take longer than this story. So Stud gives Unknown the benefit of the doubt.

Stud says, "I've seen him pick up women before. He's thick on the compliments and heavy on the free drinks. Because the one thing I know, Unknown always says, is women like free drinks."

Stud, he says, "Don't these girls know your game?"

Unknown never answers. Instead, it's, "let's check out this place." Unknown says, "I'm pretty sure this place will be crawling with chicks."

Sex addicts attract sex addicts. It's on their skin, it's in their eyes, it's in the way they dress. It's like picking out a toupee or having gaydar. "You just know," Unknown says. He says, "Within a second, I can tell if she likes to have fun."

She's the girl whose friends are all male but isn't dating any of them. They look at her like a sister, until of course she's on the verge of passing out. Then she's the last resort. Sex addicts, the female ones, they often wake up naked to discover that eight of their male friends and two guys they don't even know have pulled a train on them the night before. Unknown, he says, "They won't address the situation for fear of ruining the friendship. Instead, they go about their lives thinking how wonderful it is to be surrounded by such great guys." He says, "I wouldn't be surprised if they roofie themselves to expedite the evening."

Unknown, he's been with 124 women up to now. And the real Unknown, through the ghostly drains, says, "That sounds about right."

There are a couple laughs, one voice says, "Prove it," and then a wave of flushes as if the prisoners are at a baseball game rallying for Unknown to get to 150.

"One woman," Unknown says, "comes up to me and tells me that she can tell what type of person I am just by feeling my butt."

Stud, he says, "Is that sex addict radar? Would you call it sadar? Or saraydar?"

Unknown says, "That's a coincidence. Just by touching a woman's breasts I can tell if I want to have sex with her."

She laughs as Unknown mimics groping breasts with his two hands, palms outward. First, his hands are cupped the size of softballs. He says, "Yes." Then, they're cupped the size of baseballs. He says, "Yes." Last, his hands are flat, showing that the woman has no tits whatsoever. He says, "No. Then, Maybe."

The woman, ready to convince, says, "Turn around, I'll prove it."

Unknown does and she feels his butt, repeatedly by groping, massaging, and moving her palms up and down in a semi-quick notion. The motion of her hands, it's like a magic trick and Stud is picturing a rabbit coming out of Unknown's asshole. And the audience, the imaginary crowd at this smoke infested club, it's saying, "Ooh, magnifico!"

The groping, massaging, it's a sexual harassment charge waiting to happen. For Unknown, though, it's a mental note to buy her drinks, lots of them. He says,

"Maybe I can get her to do that same motion on my other side."

She says, "The curves in your cheeks tell me you're a sensitive person."

She says, "You're the type of person that has a wall up and you won't let anyone inside until you can trust them."

She says, "When you do let these people in, you keep them there forever."

Unknown, knowing that she's not even close, says, "How did you know?"

She smiles, stops and says, "Impressed?"

Stud rolls his eyes at this account, and wonders if this woman is ranked in the double digits.

Unknown says, "I tell her that I don't even need to feel her breasts to know that I want to nail her. She's a six foot beauty whose body is 85% legs while the rest of her is 15% lips and perky tits. Her legs, perfect stalks would wrap nicely around my waist."

"Her lips," Unknown says, "would fit nicely around my cock. Her hands, by the way they move, I wouldn't be surprised if something came out of his ass."

The woman, a sex addict like no other sex addict, reads her typical quote unquote fortune the same way psychics do. It's the same shit. That's how psychics work. That, save for Unknown, works on 90% of people. Unknown says, "Sometimes people just want someone else to tell them that everything is going to all right."

Unknown, he says, "But if you grew up with a mother who abused you, you soon learn that nothing is ever all right."

This woman, convinced that Unknown is impressed with her abilities, says, "Now, you impress me."

And Unknown, thick on the compliments and heavy on the drinks, says, "What're you drinking?"

She says, "Vodka Tonic. You buying?"

Unknown, he says, "You don't have to ask me twice." He disappears to the bar, orders up two of the same drinks, and returns.

"I invest in stocks," Unknown says. He says, "All types of stocks. I'm talking about turning a few thousand dollars into tens of thousands."

The woman, sipping from her glass, says, "Tell me what I should do with me money."

Unknown goes into his scheme, ordering drinks in the process and tipping the bartender to double the gin in her glass while laying off his, until the woman is questioning her retirement.

She says, "So I should be moving my money into the high risk fund?"

Unknown, a diligent researcher to convince all parties that he knows what he is doing, says that she should diversify her monies into high risk, low risk and international stocks. He says, "You should have gotten information on each stock so you could assess what type of return your investment will yield."

Stud says, "If Unknown spent as much time going to college or starting a business as he does researching on topics to get him laid, he may legitimately be a millionaire."

The woman, she says, "I can look up all that stuff online. Want to go back to my place so you can show me on my computer?"

He says, "Sure, I'll drive. Where do you live?"

And then the next thing the woman knows is she's riding Unknown like he's a pogo stick. He says, "Did your powers see that coming?"

He says, "Impressed?"

He says, "What type of person do you think I am now?

The woman, she was number 71. And Stud, he says, "Double digits."

Unknown became a sexaholic like most men in America. Sex addicts search for porn on the Internet and then all of a sudden, masturbating becomes history and it's sex wherever they can find it. A simple spam email message starts the addiction, Free Porn or Britney Hard Core. A click, a click, and the next thing you know you're knee deep in one dimensional vaginas. And then the next thing you know you're getting it for real.

Stud, he says, "There are men like this everywhere. Married ones who go out of their way to hide a porn stash in the garage or buried beneath old VCR tapes in the basement, all this while their wives are upstairs waiting to be given attention to."

Unknown, he says, "I'll give their wives attention."

Wives, they say that they come downstairs to find their husbands only to catch them jacking off to the computer. At first it's a surprise. Next, it's a shock. The third, fourth, eighth time it happens they have no feeling anymore.

These husbands, sitting in the dark with the only light coming from a streaming video on a 15-inch monitor, have their pants down to their ankles, and their johnsons are slowly getting harder and harder with each click. The volume is low to hide themselves from scrutiny, but loud enough to hear the faint moans and screams from their latest obsession.

"Hard core blonde gets anal."

"Best POV ever."

"Amateur video with my girlfriend and her sister."

Married men, who have Penthouse and Playboy magazines with Popular Science covers stapled on top to cover them, have wives saying how fascinated their husbands are about science.

The voices in the drainpipes, one says, "What do you think happens to Playboy Playmates after they've posed? Do you think they just get married and have babies? You never hear from them anymore."

The ghost, the other voice in the drainpipes, it says, "I think that would make a great reality show. The lives of Playmates after they've whored themselves out. It could be called, 'Whore Are They Now?'"

Then laughter traveling through until a couple toilets flush.

Step number 10) We were drawn to people who were not available to us, or who would reject or abuse us.

Unknown and Stud have been friends for years. But since he's become this way, a rabid sex fiend, Stud can't be around him that much. Namely because Stud used to be like him. Namely because Stud was him.

Stud is riding in Unknown's car en route to a club infested with college girls ready and willing. All this according to Unknown. If you ask Unknown, he says he's picked up about 40 girls here. He has used the investing guru act, Tom Cruise's manager, and one time he said he was going to donate his body to science the next day. The woman, she felt sorry for him and slept with him for his last wish.

Stud, he says, "You have to hand it to Unknown, he sure did a lot of research on donating your body to a good cause. He found organizations, printed out phony disclaimer forms, and even fake called a scientist who told him that if he had any questions, to feel free and phone."

The woman couldn't believe that this man would give up his life to help save future lives. She's now thinking that she should begin to volunteer her time as well. Unknown says, "I think I saw her one day. We made eye contact but I looked away. The next thing I knew she was gone."

Stud, he says, "She's probably in therapy right now."

Step number 9) We searched for some "magical" quality in others to make us feel complete. Other people were idealized and endowed with a powerful symbolism, which often disappeared after we had sex with them.

Unknown says, "This place has cheap pitchers of beer. Just buy a few and the next thing you know, you're buried in college ass." He says, "College hotties who ask for it by wearing small T-shirts that read, 'Save A Virgin, Ride Me.' Shirts that read, 'Innocent Until Proven Horny.'

Stud says, "I don't know how many sex addicts you know but that's all they think about. It consumes their minds and lots of times, their lives and work suffer."

Often, Unknown will scheme up plans to get laid. "It's a job," Unknown says. "But instead of getting paid, I get laid."

Unknown loves this line. So much so he finds ways to use it on people.

"You've had sex with that many women?"

Unknown then says, "It's a job. But instead of getting paid, I get laid."

"Why don't you get a real job where you can work yourself up?"

Unknown then says, "It's a job. But instead of getting paid, I get laid."

For about three months, Unknown found himself hanging out at hotel bars hitting on the women who were in town for business. He had a story and everything.

Unknown, top salesperson for a computer company. He sells software that some whiz kid created. "The program allows users to - well, I don't want to bore you," Unknown says. And that's as far as he needs to go.

Unknown, he has an expense account used for gasoline and a food per diem. He says, "I think it's around twenty five bucks but sometimes I'll go over. But I don't want to bore you with the details."

These details, meticulously plotted while Unknown peddles his music and movies online, are so specific that any question surrounding his scheme has a valid response.

"I know what you mean," a woman says. She says, "We have IT geeks everywhere at work." The hotel bar is empty and this woman is thanking God that she has someone to talk to. The first night in town she stayed in her room and watched reruns of Sex And The City. This night, one drink at the bar turns into company.

Unknown says, "What're you drinking?" He looks at the bartender and motions him for two of the same, whatever she is having. He says, "Are you married?"

The woman says that she's separated, and has been for the last four years. "He doesn't want to split the cost of divorce so we haven't actually signed papers yet," she says. "I sure the hell am not going to pay for it, so that's why it's taking so long."

Two drinks come, and Unknown says to put them on a tab. She says, "We don't have any children so there really isn't an excuse to talk to him. In fact, it's probably been around two years since I've heard from him. I'm just waiting for him to call and say, 'I am getting remarried. Want to split the divorce?' It hasn't happened yet."

Unknown, he smells the glass to discover that it's a Vodka Tonic. He says, "Why didn't you have children?"

"I'm career oriented. That's why I'm here now," she says. She picks up her glass and takes a drink. "You?"

Unknown, he tells her how his work has taken away any possibility of him settling down. "I always question my life, wondering if I should have gotten married and had children," he says. "I guess I was just born a workaholic."

He shrugs, and then looks around the bar. The woman, she smiles and places her hand on Unknown's arm. "Don't beat yourself up about working all the time. Marriage isn't for everyone."

Unknown, he says, "Yea, my colleague locked himself in our room so he could talk to his wife. I'm basically forbidden until he texts me." And by doing this, Unknown makes himself attractive. Unknown, he says, "I'm willing to sit at the bar until he finishes up with his wife." He holds up the glass and downs the rest of it.

"Well then," she says, "let's go back to my room."

The next morning, Unknown is gone from the premises, never to see this woman again.

"It's worked so many times," Unknown says. He says, "I honestly believe these women just want some action." Unknown says this to lighten the way Stud feels about him. He says, "My story is so BS, I can't believe anyone would fall for it." He says this to get a reaction. He says this to feel important.

"After all," Unknown says, "it's a job. But instead of getting paid, I get laid."

Unknown, he's been a screenwriter and movie director scouting for some actresses to appear in his next film. A film with a working title and he's waiting to hear from the city so that he can get permission to shoot. He says, "The film commission hasn't gotten back to me yet. I'm hoping to get a grant to help fund the project."

And you can bet that these women will check the papers for potential city blocks being closed down.

Unknown, auditioning women for a role that doesn't exist, courtesy of the legend of Tom Cruise or the legend of Brad Pitt. "Pitt's going to be in this movie?" Then screams and buckled knees. And Unknown, he's saying how these women are flocking to auditions. He even has a sample script he downloaded off the Internet. Unknown, he says, "I tell them the real script is secret; it's a writer's insecurity. I just read with them, and the ones that really want the role, they're rehearsing lines with me after hours."

Unknown sits at the bar looking, at people, at locations, anything to give the impression he's working. He stares at the ceilings, at stop lights and street corners. He's looking at women with interest, all to serve his purpose of Unknown, movie director. Unknown, sex addict. Unknown, scammer. And Unknown, anonymous.

Women, they say, "He's working on a film. We don't know what kind of film, but it's a film. And you'll never guess who's in it? Bah rad Pitt!"

Unknown pulls into a parking lot. Cars are scattered around and he and Stud pass a Jetta, a Ford Aspire, a beat up pick-up truck, and other cars Unknown has no interest in. He finds a spot next to a sharp looking BMW. Unknown, he says, "Park next to a nice car because if women see you near it, then in the club if they see you again, that'll stick in their minds."

Stud, he says, "What happens if they want to go for a ride?"

"You buy them drinks," Unknown says. He says, "And after a few, the only ride they wanna take is on the bologna pony."

Stud says into the drain pipes, "You may want to listen to the next part." He says, "Unknown's full of them."

A ride on the dick stick.

A ride on the cock rock.

A ride on the boner moaner.

Step number 6) We tried to bring intensity and excitement into our lives through sex, but felt ourselves growing steadily emptier.

One time Unknown tells Stud that he set up a swingers party via the Internet and made it with three husbands' wives in one night. He says, "They even knew I was nailing their wives. They were 86, 87, and 88."

Eighty six was a ten where she should have been a 34. "Flat," Unknown says. "Everything else on her was perfect. Hour glass figure, nice round hips, long stalks for legs and perfect knees. Cute smile, soft skin but her chest, her chest was like looking at two Tic Tacs on an ironing board."

Eighty seven he can't remember too well. "Never again. Yeah, I don't even want to think of that one." Then he shakes his head in disgust.

Eighty eight had boobs the size of Macy Thanksgiving Day Parade balloons. Unknown says, "I felt like I was sleeping in between globes. Imagine, her on top while you're looking up and seeing two hot air balloons hanging above you."

Stud says, "Woody Woodpecker?"

He says, "Spider-Man?"

He says, "Underdog?"

Unknown, he's saying how she'll have back problems when she gets older. Her skinny legs won't be able to hold them up too long. "She should be getting a breast reduction," he says. "That'll give her a few more years of nice, swinger action."

The swingers party was in a strip club and afterward, Unknown walked over to the main part of the club and used up all of his one dollar bills on a girl named Kiley, the girl who would be number 89.

"What's going on over there?" she asks. She moves her head left to right to get a better look. The music is bumping and she's yelling at Unknown and Unknown is leaning in close to her, his head cocked so that he can hear her. She smells like cotton candy and Unknown, for one second, inhales her scent while staring at her breasts.

He says, "Over there? It's some party." And that's all he needs to work an "in" with Kiley the dancer.

She says, "Why did you leave?"

Unknown, he says, "I saw something beautiful over here and I just had to see what was catching my eye." He closes his eyes and takes in her scent. She smiles, the glitter splayed on her body sparkling under the night.

Unknown says, "How long have you been dancing?"

She says that she got kicked out of her house for smoking pot. "I was dating this guy and that's all he did all day. I'd never done anything like that. I didn't smoke or anything," Kiley says. She says, "A couple months after dating him, I dropped out of school. He wanted to get a place together. I had to get a job so I started working at the mall. That was our deal. We both had to work so we could afford an apartment together."

The song stops and the spotlight hits the stage. The dancer on stage, walks down the steps and the disc jockey calls up the next girl.

She says, "The problem was he never got a job. He just kept smoking pot. Eventually I started smoking pot. We couldn't afford our apartment so we moved in with my dad."

Unknown, he says, "And your dad didn't mind you dropping out of school for this guy?"

A few of the swingers walk up to the stage. They pull out chairs, throw dollars on the edge and wait for the dancer to come around. One yells at the girl and the other two laugh.

Kiley leans into Unknown and says, "He did. But at the end of the day I'm his little girl."

"So he doesn't mind you doing this?" Unknown says. Kiley is topless, talking to Unknown like everything is normal. It's apparent to Unknown that she's been doing this for a while.

Kiley says, "He doesn't know. After he kicked us out for drugs, I haven't really talked to him." She looks up at the dancer on stage and whistles. She then says, "Do you want a private dance?"

Unknown smiles, goes back to the designated area with the girl, and in three minutes, the length of the song that's playing, Unknown and Kiley are making plans to hook up afterward. He says, "I don't have any pot."

She smiles, and says, "I don't do that anymore. If I knew that it would ruin my life, I wouldn't have started."

"Where do you want to meet up?" Unknown says.

"Meet me at the IHOP," she says. He does and has the biscuits and gravy while Kiley has a stack of pancakes covered with blueberries and later on for dessert, she inhales Unknown's schlong bong.

Number 89.

Stud says, "All Unknown can remember about her is that she's not even old enough to drink yet and is tight. Tight ass, tight twat, tight everything."

Through the pipes, Unknown, he says, "Thank you daddy issues. You get the assist."

Stud, adjusting himself around the toilet, says, "Now, back to the club that we were at."

The club, it's packed with college students. The place has two levels, one with a dance floor and the other with pool tables and dart boards. Music blares through the Bose speaker system, pumping out bass that pounds through Stud's heart and chest. He says, "I can't hear any lyrics, just thump, thump, thumping in my chest and head."

Unknown yells over the song, "Go buy a pitcher." Then he says, "Number 125 is right over there."

Unknown is the youngest of two boys. His brother Mike is a genius. Mike attended MIT and now works as a consultant for a Fortune 500 company in New York City. He did everything by the book; no drinking, no dating, no drugs. He did this all for the sake of career.

When Mike was away at camp, or gone each night for one of his many extracurricular activities, Unknown stayed home with their mother.

Mike says, "Why don't you do something with your life?" He constantly harasses Unknown about doing something. It's been like this since they were kids.

Unknown, he says, "My brother's an over-achiever. One of those dorky kids."

Step number 1) As adolescents, we used fantasy and compulsive masturbation to avoid feelings, and continued this tendency into our adult lives with compulsive sex.

Step number 3) We tended to become immobilized by romantic obsessions. We became addicted to the search for sex and love; as a result, we neglected our lives.

Unknown says, "If I don't talk to girls I get depressed."

Stud, he says, "You have to hand it to them, Unknown can pick up women."

Mike has been dating the same woman for years but, according to Unknown, she's not that attractive. In Unknown's mind, the best woman is a trophy one.

Number 125 is certainly a trophy. Not one of those cheesy ones given to everyone just for participating, but the huge ones that bowlers get. The ones you deserve. Unknown says, "The ones that scream 'worked for.'"

"Look at her ass," Unknown says. "Have you seen an ass like that?"

Number 125, her name is Gretchen, has black straight hair. It falls down the sides of her face, hiding her cheeks so a person doesn't see her cute dimples. Gretchen's voice is soft and she is very polite.

Unknown says, "I love the dark rimmed plastic glasses she has on."

And then it's step number 4) We sought oblivion in fantasy and masturbation, and lost ourselves in compulsive sex. Sex became a reward, punishment, distraction and time-killer.

"Man," a voice screams down the pipes. "Unknown got nailed."

"Literally," a ghost says. And then a flush.

15.

The stories around the prison have become what are called the drainpipe story sessions. Each prisoner looks forward to the sessions as the stories have become a form of expression. The prisoners use this time to one up each other, bull shit a story idea they're working on, and more importantly, cope with their mistakes.

Just like the relationships that Stud talks about, these stories, they're filled with facts and fictions.

Unknown, he wants each inmate to feel like he's contributed to society. Something about having a purpose in life, no matter what type of life you choose.

Since the stories began, Stud has become more open, more anxious about the stories he tells. And the more and more he hears others' tales, the more he wants them to know about him. Yelling in a toilet, although far from what he had ever imagined, has now been what he looks forward to.

Activity hour in the prison is now referred to as poop time, or pee time. Or whatever it is they have to do about their bowels.

A flush is heard, then a bad joke, and then Stud goes, continuing his life's story to anyone willing to listen. Regardless of the audience, Stud finds this time therapeutic. For good measure, however, Stud, he asks how many prisoners are listening. The regulars, they're all ears.

Stud, he says, "The carpet in my living room is slightly worn from me sitting every day. It's a faded tan, a little lighter than its original color. Picture the original hue with the sun shining on it. That's the color it is now. If it gets any lighter there will have be new carpet."

Sitting in the same position for so long Stud learned to meditate. Often, he'll open the windows in the apartment to let in the surrounding noises. Outside the wind is blowing, the leaves are rustling, car doors are closing, a little two year old is crying and asking for her binky, and sirens are blaring and then fading out. These are all noises that help calm Stud.

Couples, walking back to their homes, and their friends are saying about them, "Aren't they so cute together?"

"My mind, it pictures things like the sun, a mountain range, a beautiful woman. All this while I'm inhaling deeply and exhaling just as deep," Stud says. He says, "My eyes are closed, my body is calm and my arms are resting to the sides of my torso. Nothing shakes my concentration."

At the forefront of everything is Stud's condition, how to accept it and play with the cards he has been dealt.

The commercials, they tell you to live a normal life by taking their product to treat herpes. On the commercials, the actors with herpes are horseback riding, playing beach volleyball and kayaking.

Stud, he says, "I don't do any of those things."

In a lot of bars, there's a picture with a bunch of dogs sitting around a card table, with cigars, poker chips and ashtrays and the caption, it reads, "Life is like a poker hand, either bluff your way through or fold."

Stud says, "Me, I plan not to fold. Why would I?" He says, "My life is not that bad. There are people starving, but they don't have herpes. There are people out there with nothing, but nothing means no herpes."

Stud shakes his head, with the window to his right rattling from the gust of wind. He focuses on his life, taking into consideration what Lydia tells him. She says, "Kick your ball into her stomach. Take control of your life."

Even with the wind causing the window to move, Stud's eyes are still closed. He says, "My life isn't that bad. I have a job, I have a car, I have friends." He says, "There are people worse off than me. A single mother of four on welfare. She's worse off than me. A husband who just lost his job with a family to feed and a mortgage to pay. He's worse off than me. A panhandler living on the streets. He's worse than me." Saying these things seems to calm Stud a bit.

Before Stud falls into a deep trance, the phone rings. Stud knows the person calling is Lydia. It's always Lydia. She calls every day around this time if she's not sitting on Stud's patio staring out into the parking lot. At this time, there is no boy kicking a ball into a girl's stomach. There is no couple unloading groceries from a car. There is nothing but parked cars and the occasional squirrel running by.

Stud, he says, "Hello."

"You're still sulking, aren't you?"

Stud stops and uncrosses his legs to better relax himself on the floor. He leans back so his body hits the couch. His body is inclined at a 110 degree angle and his ass is sliding forward, wearing out even more of the already worn carpet.

"Hello?" he says again into the phone.

Lydia says, "You're not still sulking, are you?"
Stud, he says, "I haven't been, but OK."

Lydia, on the other line, she says, "You need to take charge of your life." This is the same song and dance she preaches every day when she calls. It's almost as if someone has recorded their conversation and plays it back each day, like a game show at the same hour. She says, "Stop sulking and take control."

Stud closes his eyes and lets Lydia give her pitch. Lydia says, "Do something you would never do in your life."

Stud says, "Huh?"

"Go out and do something you would never do in your life," she says. Her logic is to go and do something so uncharacteristic of Stud that it makes him realize that he's not that person.

Stud says to himself, "I could go kayaking, or horseback riding, or play beach volleyball." He doesn't want to stop her momentum. Especially when Lydia is being philosophical. Stud believes that Lydia counseling him is a way she copes with her own co-morbidities. He has yet to figure her out, and hasn't tried as he has been dwelling on his own illness.

"Go out and buy leather pants," Lydia says. She says, "Go out and buy a vest, a sweater vest or something." Once Stud sees that there is no end in sight, he jumps into the conversation.

Stud says, "You want me to feel unlike myself? With leather pants and a sweater vest, I'll feel like one of the Village People if he had a makeover by Mr. Rogers."

Lydia laughs and snorts at the same time. Then, she says, "Go out and bungee jump."

Stud says, "No way. My luck the cord will break. And what's left on the ground will be little bits of herpes."

Every recommendation that Lydia throws out, Stud offers up his own response.

She says, "Go serve breakfast at a kitchen." It's almost as if she is reading these passages from books. Stud envisions a stack of books in front of Lydia. Some are open to certain pages while others are bookmarked, ready to be used. He visualizes the pages highlighted throughout. Stud says, "Possibly, but then I'll have to get up early in the morning."

Even though Stud can do any of these things Lydia mentions, he comes up with ways and excuses not to. The conversation has now become a game, a game where Lydia reads passages from a book and Stud uses his wit for a response.

She says, "Go dancing."

Stud says, "Don't think so. Have you seen me dance?"

"Go rob a bank."

"What?" Stud is taken off guard. "Score one for Lydia," he says to himself.

Lydia, she says, "I'm kidding. Go out and get a haircut. A manicure. A nail buff or something. A massage. A.."

"That's enough," Stud says.

Lydia, she wants Stud to feel unlike himself. Stud says, "I already do. Remember, I have herpes." Outside the window, Stud can hear the little boy kicking his ball in the air. He stands and walks out on the balcony and watches.

"But you don't feel unlike yourself," Lydia says. She says, "You feel normal now. You felt different when you first found out. Now, you've adjusted to it and now you're normal."

Anonymous

Stud watches the boy kick the ball a few times. Before he gets a headache, he sits back against the couch and stretches out his legs.

Lydia, she says, "Go do something out of the ordinary so you can feel weird again to help you get back to how you were before you were infected."

Lydia, this philosophical woman, plays mind games with Stud. Her voice, crystal clear, is nothing but a sound coming in Stud's ear. He's in a cave and he hears her voice. It's trying to show him the way out. All this while his leather pants are soaked with sweat and his sweater vest is tight around his stomach.

Stud says, "Like what?"

Lydia says, "I don't know. That's something you have to come up with. Go to a psychic or something. I don't know. Just make sure it's your decision." She tells him to quit feeling sorry for himself. She says, "When you do something out of the ordinary, you'll realize how silly you are and you'll go back to your life."

"A psychic?" Stud says. "Like a fortune teller or something?"

Unknown, through the pipes, he says, "I know someone like that. She's very impressive." He says, "She can tell what type of person you are by touching your ass."

Lydia, she says, "Whatever. That's something you have to decide."

The last time Stud made a decision, it was to stay or go. He stayed. And what happened? Prime rib with a side of herpes.

And what happened? A three month gig with a side of herpes.

And what happened? He's now wearing leather pants and a sweater vest.

This lack of going out and doing anything, it's a reflection on that one decision. Stud questions his actions each day, hoping that the simplest task doesn't result in something like chlamydia.

Lydia, she says, "Go out a dye your hair."

And Stud, he's throwing back the excuses. "My hair doesn't need to be dyed. I'm not in a punk rock band." Once again, this game show continues on.

Lydia, she says, "Go out and learn another language."

Stud envisions Lydia highlighting each recommendation as she says them. He says, "I don't plan on leaving the country any time soon. I'm not dating a Spanish girl anytime soon. Yo tengo herpes-o. Muy mal."

And then Lydia, in Stud's head, she flips the page to the next bookmarked passage.

"Go take an origami class." Then she highlights. Stud, he says, "Why do I want to learn how to fold paper?"

She says, "Go out and do something that will totally surprise you. Do something like that." Then she says, "Go and buy a Hummer."

The wind gusts and slams the window against the building. The noise startles Stud. He turns to look behind him and sees the window shaking from the impact. He sits for a second, his body again relaxed. There are parked cars outside with a few squirrels running amok. He sits straight up with his back against the couch and listens to Lydia's voice talk him through.

She says, "Go out and take a cooking class."

Stud says, "I'll do something."

And then Lydia, stopping the page turning and highlighting, says, "I'm proud of you."

Stud, into the drain pipes, says, "Me? I'm out of the cave and the sun is shining. Me? I'm squatting in front of my toilet yelling at the top of my lungs."

"What are you in for?" a voice in the drains says.

Stud, he says, "I did something." And then he flushes.

16.

There's a horoscope that reads: "What if accidents are no accident and jokes are no joke? If life is played out in metaphors, what does a recent occurrence say about you? Looking for meaning brings revelation."

Sex, it's impulsive. It's an addiction. Much of it is due to childhood experiences. It could be from something traumatic, like being raped by a relative. It could be from sexual abuse from a boyfriend. Regardless of the source, the result, it's what is staggering. For people to act out sexually, they must look back at how they got to that point - pornography.

Unknown says, "Each second more than three thousand dollars is being spent on pornography. Each second, almost 30,000 Internet users view porn."

When you think of the Internet, companies such Google, Facebook, Amazon and eBay come to mind. Unknown, he says, "The reality? Pornography brings in more revenue than all those sites combined." Throw in Netflix and there aren't enough streaming movies to watch in a year than there are adult films.

Porn addiction, it can derive from an emotional opening that allows pornography to take charge. Unknown says, "A porn addiction can be harder to break than a cocaine addiction." And with the yearly revenues, with more than $3.5 billion being from adult movies and $2.8 billion from Internet porn, it doesn't seem like there is an end in sight.

How do you know if you have an addiction to porn? You're masturbating more and more, thinking of unrealistic scenarios you seen in movies. There are five stages of porn, which begin at early exposure and culminate in acting out sexually.

Unknown, he says, "I know first hand what this feels like." He says to each prisoner, through the pipes, yelling at each individually, "Speaking of first hand, remember when you first masturbated?"

According to Unknown, masturbation is where it all began. The feeling of something changing, changing you from a person of innocence to a person of addiction to a person of interest. How did that time come? Why did that time come? The first time, masturbating, figuring out that your penis has more of a purpose than to simply urinate.

Unknown, he says, "You flick it, you twang it like a whammy bar on an Ibanez guitar, you push it down between your legs just because, until you finally yank it when something, something, white, sticky and milky shoots out."

Boys, discovering something new with this pot of gold, they hope that when they first come that don't need medical attention.

"The first time," Unknown says, "you're standing above the toilet bowl trying to force out urine. All this while you're losing your harden. From your penis, instead of the clear or faint yellow stream you're used to, a thick, white warm drip of snot covers the head of your dick."

Each prisoner, he's hesitant with his reply, embarrassed possibly of what the others will think.

Eventually, after hearing Unknown tell stories of mastering the skin flute, the inmates finally begin to play along. Unknown encourages each prisoner to come forward and talk, talk about the first time.

And one at a time, each inmate shares his story.

Tex, he says, "I was twelve, watching a movie called Night Patrol with my older brother. This woman, her boobs were gigantic. My penis," he says, hearing slight giggles from the others echoing through the drains, "my penis began to harden. I didn't know what to do. I thought I was growing a third leg, a leg that didn't go full term."

A couple prisoners laugh, and one voice says, "My hard-on was so big I looked like R2 friggin' D2."

Tex, he says, "I kept trying to make it smaller with my hand. I kept moving it, back and forth, side to side, it felt weird." Tex, lying on the couch, his hand disappeared in his shorts, the blanket, once on the floor now over his body, covering up his waist, he continues to move it, so much so, there's a shot outside the head.

"I flinched a bit and ran to the bathroom," Tex says. He says, "I thought I had to go pee." That first time triggered a weekly touch session until Tex was pleasuring himself in the shower on Friday nights, which was shower night in his house. He took half hour showers with his mother's conditioner being used as a lubricant. After a few minutes, Tex didn't know what was conditioner and what was come.

Tex says, through his empty bowl, "Some of it probably got in my hair." Simultaneously, the rest of the guys cut a look to their respective toilet, and a laugh is heard coming from Unknown's direction.

Unknown says, "Is that why your hair is so shiny?"

The inmates, they listen as Tex regains his position on his bed. Then there's silence. His eyes water up, and he thinks about how he became a child molester.

Unknown says, in between a couple flushes, "Anyone else? Who's next?"

Tom stands, collects himself and clears his throat. He positions himself in front of his toilet, gripping the bowl tightly and perching his head above the rim. Until now, Tom had been silent in regard to the drain pipe sessions. His alternate state keeps him separate from the other prisoners, who like to talk about similar topics.

Tom, he says, "I used to take my dad's Playboy magazines into the bathroom and lock the door. I would pull my pants down so my boner would stand erect, straight out, pointing at the naked women on the pages."

Tom's eyes move left to right as if he has a secret. He says, "Then I would stick my penis into the pages where the woman's boobs were. Or her vagina was." Tom, he would jam his boner into the paper until it hurt. He says, "That's when I discovered blue balls."

There are a couple snickers through the pipes. They sound eerie and, at times, they frighten Tom. Tom's real name is unknown, and was given the symbolic name Tom because he was arrested for peeping in women's bedroom windows. Tome, he says, "I was caught in a tree of a woman's yard, standing on a branch with my pants down."

Standing on the branch, his back nestled in between a crevice in the trunk, Tom was masturbating to an undressing victim until he triggered on the grass by the tree. He says, "Damn dog, the fucker kept barking at me."

Standing there, his back against the trunk, his pants around his ankles and the dog, it was staring up at him. Its teeth were out and its bark was informing its owner that there was a peeping Tom in the tree. Tom, he says, "Get the fuck away from me," as his hand stroked his penis to squeeze out all the come.

Tom says, in regard to almost getting paper cuts on his penis from magazines, "Those blue balls hurt like hell. I didn't do it as much. After a while, I finally started touching myself, fondling myself until I got so excited that something came out."

He says, "I thought I was dying. I was only a kid, not even a teen yet, and I didn't know what it was. But it felt good."

There is a brief silence, and the only thing the detainees could hear are random flushes around the prison. "I masturbated so much it got me locked up," Tom says. He says, "That's it. There's nothing else."

Nose, he also knows how to masturbate. Nose slides up to the toilet; he's ready to give his story. For full effect, he pulls down his pants down to his ankles and yanks a stretch of toilet paper from its roll.

"In grade school," Nose says, "I was playing hide and seek with some friends. It was my turn to hide so I ran upstairs and searched for the perfect hiding place." Nose takes the wad of toilet paper, wraps it around his penis like a mummy, and begins stroking himself.

He says, "I found the bathroom in the master bedroom. This was at my friend's house and we weren't allowed in his parent's room." Nose, he sneaks into the bathtub, closing the curtain behind him.

Propped up with one hand against his toilet's bowl, Nose gets himself off with his other, using the dry toilet paper into it irritates his penis. Nose, he says, "My friend's brother and his girlfriend must have been there because a few moments later, they came into the bathroom and started kissing."

From the bathtub, behind the curtain, Nose hears a combination sound of slurping and panting. He slides the curtain to get a better look and sees that the girlfriend is sitting on the sink's counter with her legs spread eagle.

The boyfriend is pushed in between her legs dry humping her and the vanity at the same time. The vanity's cabinet doors push back and forth into the unit at a pace that escalates as the breathing and moaning heighten.

Nose, telling this story, masturbates faster into the toilet paper. His knees begin to shake as he ferociously whacks off like he is teaching it a lesson. He says, "I saw the boyfriend whip out his penis through his jeans, pull down his girlfriend's panties and slide it into her. I had no idea where his penis went, thinking that it was sliding under her."

Nose, innocent until proven horny, looks down at his own penis, his adolescent hairless penis, and sees that it begins to grow into adulthood. The girlfriend's moans, mixed with a series of "yea, yea, yea," and "right there, right there, right there," excites Nose to full potential.

He says, "This was the first time I experienced sex of any time. I honestly thought the only people to have sex were married couples." Nose's knees push down into the cell's concrete floor, and his wrist's motion is like a machine against his penis.

Nose, he says, "I watched the boyfriend as his body began to deflate, his head fall back farther, and his mouth open up like he was trying to catch popcorn into hit." He says, "All the while the girlfriend was moaning until all of a sudden, everything stopped."

The bathroom's mirror, it fogs up before Nose's very eyes. Both boyfriend and girlfriend are catching their breath and Nose, he's aping the movement with his own body into his hand. He says, triggering into the wad of toilet paper around his penis, "My hand was my girlfriend and I wanted to see if I had my own popcorn catching face."

Nose's warm come blasts the toilet paper and bounces back onto the head of his penis. His body convulses and his eyes close shut and his mouth, it opens, ready to catch flying popcorn.

He says into the bowl, "I did, and it was the greatest feeling I've ever had. And the best thing was I ended up winning the game."

Nose, he says, "Till this day, my friend has no idea where I was hiding. And his brother, he has no clue that I ever saw him having sex. Frankly, up until I landed in here, every time I saw his brother it was weird."

Nose removes the damp toilet paper and tosses it into the trash can. He says, "Whenever I saw him, I imagined throwing popcorn into his mouth. God forbid we went to a movie together. That would've been brutal."

Nose stands and pulls up his pants. Then he bends down and says into the bowl, "Thank you for listening. I hope all of your popcorn catching faces are as good as my friend's brother's."

Each prisoner, in his cell, semi-hard from the story, opens his mouth and closes his eyes. All at once, the prison sees a popcorn catching contest in the making. Unknown, he says, "I've seen almost 150 'O' faces."

Some inmates laugh, some still have their mouths open, and others, they're flushing the result of their "O" faces down the toilet, courtesy of Nose's story. Loads of DNA are flushing through the pipes, the same pipes the detainees use as communication sources.

From keeping a chart of how long boners are to Ambiguous's story about how he and his best friend Bobby used to stand in front of each other, naked and wank each other off. He says, "His stuff would hit my stomach and mine would hit his. We did it three times a week."

Ambiguous thought he was pregnant one time when the splash of semen covered up his belly button. He kept it a secret for two weeks until he finally confessed to his mother. His mother, shocked by what he heard, spanked him and grounded him for two months. During this grounding Ambiguous stayed in his room without any source of entertainment.

"It was like a prison," he says, comparing the silence and loneliness to his current situation.

After their stories, after the laughter dies down, the feeling is a comfortable one. They've since shared something private about themselves, something that Unknown calls trusting someone. Unknown, he says, "Now, we all trust each other. Why would you share something intimate with someone if you don't trust that person?"

Unknown, preaching into the bowl so he can cope with his irrelevancy, says, "People don't go up to strangers and say they have cancer. They don't, because they don't trust those people."

He says, "And since you told me your stories, I'll tell you mine."

17.

Before Unknown became a sexaholic, he was a masturbator. He was king of Internet porn, often downloading hundreds of pictures a week. His computer would have landed into the Adult Video Hall of Fame if it hadn't eventually crashed.

Each picture, examined and tested by the frequency in which Unknown got an erection, is saved onto his hard drive. He says, "It's as if my penis indecisive."

The photos, coming at him by the dozens, are high quality and ready for download. Unknown, he right clicks and saves into a folder. He does this at rapid speed, right clicking and saving until he is knee deep in one dimensional vaginas.

While he posts CDs online, his breaks consists of adult websites that offer free trial passes, in which he spends the majority of the passes saving pictures on his hard drive. Every day, there is an email into his inbox saying, "Your trial membership is almost expired. Don't wait any longer or you'll no longer have access." And Unknown, he's right clicking and saving, right clicking saving, into a folder designated for naked women.

One picture is of a woman spread eagle. Her bush, it's unshaven and it looks like an Afro. A throwback photo that never gets old. Anonymous, he says, "Now I know what Willis was talking about."

Right click, save.

There's a woman with soapy tits. The bubbles barely cover her nipples and the sponge she's holding is being squeezed tightly. Suds are falling down her forearm. Her smile, it's seductive and her eyes are bright blue. It's almost as if this shot was planned ahead of time. The photographer, it's as if he said, "OK, now be naked."

In the shower, on the soap ledge, is a rubber ducky waiting to be played with. This model, smiling in the buff for a paycheck, she'll forever go down as a right click, save type of girl.

A photo of a woman with her favorite dildo, a blue one the length of a baseball bat. Unknown, he's says, "Home run." The next picture has the dildo going deep and her mouth is now open and her eyes are closed. If you ever play the game where there are two seemingly identical photos and you have to tell the differences, this game would end in "mouth," "eyes," "disappearing dildo," and "come stain."

Right click, save.

There are two women pretending to be roommates. Roommates who, aside from sharing rent, share each other in a friendly tickle fight. Unknown says, "How realistic is that?" His penis, it's in the upright position waiting to played with.

One roommate, her nipples are sticking out like the room is cold. Unknown, he says, "Maybe the apartment is rent controlled. Well played landlord, well played."

Right click, save.

A picture, it's of a woman with her midget boyfriend. This tall woman with a three foot six inch midget. Anonymous says, "He looks like Jack climbing the beanstalk."

Right click, save.

There are thousands of pictures. Right click, save. Right click, save.

There is one with a woman on all fours, her ass at a boomerang angle and her head, it's cocked to the left with fucked out lazy eyes. Her back is dipped so her round ass takes up most of the picture, and her vagina is saying, "Open for business." Her panties, they're slung around her right calf, a red frilly thing. And Unknown, his pants are down around his waist and he's stroking while right click, saving. Save as, OnFours, into the folder of naked women.

Unknown says, "I have about ten thousand porn pictures downloaded." He's addicted. "I can email you one a day for 27 years."

Anonymous, trying not to eye Unknown's junk, says, "Twenty seven fucking years!

At once, the ghosts in the pipes say, "Then do it. Email us a picture a day."

There's a woman giving a man head. All that's seen is a brain of hair covering up a man's mid section. The series of pictures, if put together, is a nice head bob with her lips wrapped around the man's pecker. Unknown places the pictures in his animation software and soon after he has a looped blow job. He says, "I always get a hard-on with this one. Look at the curls in the woman's hair. Sexy."

Anonymous, his pants now unzipped, is waiting for the photo that makes him go pantless.

The next photo, it's of a woman eating out another woman. There is juice seeping out the side of her mouth. The woman getting eaten out, she's leaning back, spread eagle and her arms are behind her, hands planted to prop herself up.

Hundreds of pictures. Thousands of pictures. Twenty seven years of pictures.

Then, a Lauryn Hill CD for $5 dollars, no reserve. Email the seller with questions. Shipping is a standard $3 dollar fee anywhere in the United States but it's $5 dollars overseas. Oh, and by the way, check out my other auctions.

The CD is courtesy of Christina Rollins. Christina, many miles away, is trying to get approved for a credit card at a department store. She gets declined and the clerk tells her that she can get her credit report for free within 30 days just for filling out the application. The clerk, she says, "But just by filling this out, you get a ten percent discount on anything in the store."

Christina looks at the pile of clothes in her possession. She thinks which shirts she can buy and which ones have to go back to the racks. She thinks she has a shopping problem being denied, and now she's wondering if she should put all of the clothes back on the racks.

Christina Rollins doesn't like rock music.

Christina Rollins doesn't like country music.

Christina Rollins only listens to Rap and R&B but, according to Unknown, Christina has a diverse interest in music as well as movies. He says, "She's a big fan of opera and Kid Rock."

Now, Christina Rollins can't buy the $80 dollar pair of boots she saw in the window. All because her credit report is sub par. But with some counseling, she could be on the fast track to understanding the value of having good credit. The clerk, she says, "Those eighty dollar boots, ten percent off that and they're only around seventy two bucks."

Unknown, his stack of VHS tapes are stopped at the parts that show nudity. Salma Hayek paused, naked in front of Antonio Banderas. There's Tara Reid naked. There's Kari Wuhrer naked, in numerous movies. There's Poppy Montgomery in a side shot. There's Nicole Kidman's naked body reflecting off the mirror. Unknown says, "You see her ass and in the mirror, it's full frontal."

All of them are perfectly set to pop into the VCR at the time skin is shown.

All of them satisfy Unknown at three in the afternoon.

All of them he's used as a means to get off more than a dozen times each.

His masturbation techniques, he says, are one of a kind. "Try taking a sock, filling it up with jelly and putting it into the microwave for a minute." He says, "It feels like a real vagina."

Anonymous, his boner super hard for a picture of a red headed natural, is using his own method of masturbating.

Unknown says, "Seriously, use jelly."

Anonymous, stroking to the picture, says, "Grape jelly or strawberry jelly?" He masturbates faster until a wad of come shoots on the keyboard. His body pants hard, and his cottonmouth forces him to swallow. He says, "Does your penis smell like grapes?"

Anonymous grabs a towel and wipes down the keyboard. Then, he right clicks and saves. He says, "Poor sock. A chance to be something in life but now is stained with semen and jelly. A sock puppet maybe. How about covering a ball player's foot? But no, you're a fucking masturbation tool."

Unknown says, "Should've went with the sock. Could've felt like that red head. I would've used strawberry for her."

When Unknown is at the grocery store, Anonymous imagines him walking down the aisles to the main register holding a pair of socks and a jar of jelly. People see him walking, straight to the front in a quick manner so that no one will ask questions. They see him and say to themselves, "A pair of socks and a jar of jelly?" And thoughts, they go through each customer's mind like it's a riddle.

A science project perhaps?

Something for the kid when he goes to camp?

Through the pipes, a ghost says, "No, it's to masturbate because, according to Unknown, it feels like a real vagina." And then there is laughter.

A sock filled with jelly, nuked for a minute, it feels like a real vagina. Ready in sixty seconds, this homemade vagina, spinning around the microwave on top of the carousel.

Then another CD is sold online.

Then a DVD is sold. During the auction, it was dueled by two gentlemen who have yet to see the movie. Back and forth, the bid went up fifty cents, then another fifty cents, then again, then again until one finally ended it by bidding forty dollars more.

Sold, to jkkkk21 for $52 dollars. Please add $3 dollars for shipping. Oh, and by the way, check out my other auctions.

Unknown, he says, "Try taking baby oil, dousing your hands with it, cupping your hands together like you're praying, inserting your penis and then stroking." He says, "It's a shaved vagina."

Anonymous says, "Praying to the masturbation gods." He stands up and walks to the kitchen, grabs the

Extra Virgin Olive Oil and says, "Will this work?" On the computer, there is a barely legal brunette in a private school outfit. Her hair is in pigtails and her socks up pulled up to her knees.

Once again, his pants go down and he says, "Praying to Johnson & Johnson. Johnson & Johnson for Unknown's johnson." He quickly whacks it until he triggers on the floor. The olive oil gets in the tip of his penis and it burns, forcing him to wince.

After he recovers, he says to Unknown, "I picture you promoting baby oil for different purposes than intended. You're on a billboard and you're sitting naked with a bottle of baby oil next to you." He wipes off the oil and presses the arrow to expose the next photo.

Unknown masturbates using the two fingers method. He says, "Take your index finger and your middle finger of each hand, make the letter V. Grab your dick with these four fingers." Unknown says, "Good fake fuck. No real vagina, no shaved vagina, just a good fake fuck."

Then, an email telling Unknown his free membership is about to expire. Please pay to continue service. A URL is included for easy process. If the URL doesn't work, be sure to copy and paste it directly into the browser. If you're still having problems, then please call this number.

A CD is sold, this one a country one.

A DVD is sold, this one a musical.

Unknown, he jacks off holding a magnifying glass in front of his penis. "He says, I'm a black guy I guess." He does this to the next photo, a young petite co-ed killing time in between studying. He says, "White college girls like black guys. They don't need to go to college to learn about that." Then he triggers on the carpet. Combined, the two have shot loads of come.

Anonymous, he says, "Don't get the magnifying glass under the sun. Ouch, burnt like ants."

Unknown, he right clicks and saves and the next photo comes on the screen. He says, "Try jacking off with the numb hand method. Sit on your hand until it goes numb, then masturbate and it feels like someone else is doing it."

Anonymous says, "Shake my hand and then feel your hand when it's numb. If it feels the same, then don't masturbate with a numb hand." The photo on the computer screen is of twins, both naked with snow boots on. There is snow on the ground and the only thing accommodating their boots is a pair of sleds. Unknown and Anonymous, they look at each other, sit on their hand and then jack off to the twins.

Anonymous says, "Double your pleasure, double your fun." And then they wipe up their come.

The masturbation methods, they never stop. Unknown, he rubs his hands together really fast until they heat up, and jacks off. "Hot damn!" Unknown says. He says, "A spicy Mexican vagina." And right away, Anonymous searches for a hot Latina to masturbate to.

Unknown uses the banana method.

Unknown uses the melon method.

Unknown uses the sock filled with jelly method again.

Then, Unknown, he's at the grocery store buying more bananas, more melons, more jars of jelly and more socks. All of these items moving down the conveyor belt while the teenager working the cash register is wondering how many more pieces of fruit his son might need at camp.

Anonymous, he says, "Anything else?" He's rubbing his hands so fast together they're starting to burn.

The mature Latina on the screen, her bush can be mistaken for Don King's hair. When he's full potential and his hands are on fire, Anonymous jacks it so fast that he screams in pain. The scream turns to enjoyment and a few seconds later, he's coming more than he's ever come before.

Unknown, he smiles, waits until Anonymous cleans up and says, "I have more ways to ejaculate than anyone on this earth. Take a balloon, fill it up with marbles and then jam it up your ass -"

Anonymous says, "That's all I can handle." His penis is limp and the hole is burning from the multiple ejaculations mixed with Extra Virgin Olive Oil.

Embarrassed to say, Anonymous used to be like Unknown. He used to be Unknown, save for the extravagant productions while he soiled his sheets, his carpets and his computer monitor. Not to mention socks and pieces of fruit.

When this gets old, Unknown moves to his mattress, drilling holes the size of his erection and filling them up with baby oil. He uses a lubricated condom and ruins his mattress over the course of a month or so, often drilling up to six holes on each side. By the end of it all, his mattress looks like a cocoon of some sort.

His mattresses have seen better days. Unknown, he's seen better days. He says, "We all want to matter. That's why we act this way."

Unknown used to masturbate like crazy. Now he does it for real with women he meets online, at bars, anywhere they hang out.

"It's a job," Unknown says. "But instead of getting paid, I get laid."

"Libby," Anonymous says, "this chick is crazy. She used to be a dancer for me but she ended up in the armed forces and is somewhere in San Diego right now."

Unknown and Anonymous used to have sex with her at different times, unbeknownst to her that the two know each other. According to Libby, she was getting away with something.

What she didn't know was Unknown and Anonymous would compare stories. Unknown would say he was seeing her on Friday and then Anonymous would call Libby and ask if she wanted to go out on Friday night, just so the two could hear her come up with excuses.

Libby can't because she has to work early on Saturday.

Libby can't because she's got plans with the girls tonight.

Libby can't because, well, she just can't.

The two would do this all the time. In between dates and phone calls, more CDs and DVDs are sold. Unknown, he's packing a disc for shipment, watching the television and screaming, "What is Business Law?"

And Anonymous, pants down around his ankles, is masturbating to a porn star riding a cock reverse cowgirl in a POV video rated five out of five stars by 6,000 users.

When Libby said she was moving to join the Navy, Unknown and Anonymous ended their little game. When Unknown was at Libby's, Anonymous stopped by. "I was in the neighborhood so I decided to drop by."

Libby, she looked around for an excuse and said she was on her way out the door to go to work. The door was cracked open with Libby's body blocking any view to inside her house. Then, Unknown, entered the picture, the door flinging open, and said, "Ready?"

And Unknown and Anonymous left, with Unknown jumping in the passenger side of the car and the two taking off. Libby, on the other hand, stood in embarrassment and moved to San Diego. The two, they haven't seen her since.

Now, every day, Anonymous is sitting in his living room on the carpet assessing his life.

Lydia, she's proud of Anonymous, for taking control of his life.

Unknown, he's now banged 150 women, give or take.

Unknown, he has thousands of CDs he has to sell.

Unknown, he has thousands of DVDs he has to sell.

Unknown, his favorite masturbation technique is using toothpaste, another object slowly moving down the conveyor belt, one that the teenager ringing it up can understand if Unknown's boy is in fact away at camp. Unknown, he says, "Plaster your balls and hard-on with toothpaste. Wait like 30 seconds and when your penis begins to burn, slowly whack it. It's orgasmic."

Every time Unknown brushes his penis, afterward, it smells like stale mint. The smeared teal colored putty like substance stretches from his waist to the head of his penis. And his hand, it's sticky from the toothpaste.

Unknown, says, "The toothpaste burns your dick man."

Anonymous says, "Do nine out of ten dentists recommend?"

Although Unknown's pornography is well kept on his hard drive in the folder named TAXES, he hasn't visited them in a while. His only computer activities are now solely concentrated on selling, selling, selling so that he can make money, money, money.

Unknown says, "I still like me a good fake fuck every now and then." He's on his second mattress and six hundredth sock. His socks, co-mingled together because many are without pairs, wait until the days they are called into the game.

His toothpaste supply looks as if it belongs in a dental office. Rows and rows of tubes lined up in his bathroom closet.

Unknown's pantry looks like a grocer's fresh fruit section. Even when the bananas turn brown, he's justifying his actions by saying the vagina is old and worn. All of these actions, they bring him back to his childhood. Whenever he was feeling irrelevant, his mother would buy him something. He just wants to feel wanted; he just wants to feel taken.

18.

Sex addicts are just people who really hate being bored. If these people had something to do, they wouldn't be sticking their pee pee's in every woman they see. If these people had something to do, they wouldn't be opening their legs for every smooth talker that came their way. Give them something to do and maybe, just maybe, these sex addicts won't be so horny. So how do you stop a sex addict? You slap a sexually transmitted disease on him.

Stud, he says, "I met Unknown at a strip club, my strip club. The one I own. Dancers." It's up Brady Street and then a left on 65th St. Go up a couple blocks and you can't miss it. The building has no windows and the front door has a one way see through mirror fit perfectly over it. There's a spider web shatter in the center of it when a drunk patron through a chair at it, but other than that, it's in tip top condition.

You can always tell where the strip clubs are in your city. The businesses surrounding it are usually dancer friendly. Stores such as tanning salons, liquor stores and costume shops for any holiday, they entice you with their neon signs high above the ground. Stud works regularly with these owners, exchanging business for free advertisement. Stud, he says, "Thanks to the liquor store, men picking up 30 packs have a reason to stop in. Thanks to the tanning beds, my girls don't have to go far in between shifts."

Stud says, "Until the drunk patron pays for the door, it'll always be like that." From the outside, the building looks like an adult book store. The plainness is mysterious to people. Although Stud has no interest in books and inflatable fuck dolls, the girls that dance for him make for an interesting lifestyle.

Dancers, it's the required distance away from churches and schools, something that's underlined in the zoning laws. Five hundred or so feet away so that when people drive by it, from the street, it's almost a dead giveaway about what type of atmosphere belongs inside it.

According to Stud, there are two types of atmospheres that people see – adult video store and strip club. Just like people, Dancers is as anonymous as ever.

The first atmosphere is filled with books covering anal, vaginal, and oral sexual pleasures, and magazines involving every type of masturbation secret and blow up dolls hanging from the ceiling for display. There are rooms filled with horny old men masturbating until their DNA is splashed across the floor, their legs are wide open and their pants are unbuckled and down around their legs. Insects, they're running for the darkness as the porno on the screen flickers its blue and yellow lights. Sounds of moaning and saliva sticking to skin exit the rooms. There is a 20-something-year old hippie working the register who is dealing pot out of the store. He uses the code word "freak" for anyone interested in dealing. This atmosphere, according to Stud, brings a different type of creepy.

Stud, through the pipes, he says, "Or my atmosphere, with girls twirling around on poles with little miniature treasure chest shaped purses, some covered in stickers and others see through as if they're going through airport security. There are enormous men with sleeves rolled up to show their mammoth guns wearing shirts that read SECURITY, while waitresses are walking around with as little clothing without being naked. And me, Unknown, and a few regulars who have nothing else going on in their lives."

There are wall to wall televisions blaring the 24-hour sports channels with one set always tuned into a music channel showing videos. Stud says, "This TV is for Lou, the grandfather of the strip club. He's been coming around before most of these girls were born." Lou's bar stool is turned to face the television and whenever the Closed Caption posts its dialog, it often gets confused from the hip vernacular of the hottest artists on the charts.

Regulars, they sit at the stage, their dollars stacked to the ceiling and they're looking to see who's going up soon. The DJ, he stands talking to a few girls on deck, finding music for them to dance to. And the regulars, they're getting more dollars out to accommodate two songs and a private dance. "That girl, she's just outta high school," a regular says to a man next to him. He says, "I have pubic hair older than her." The front of his pants is stained with alcohol or sweat or urine or come, whichever reason he decides to go with that night.

Stud used to be like Unknown, a sex addict whose only thought in the morning was to get laid. Stud was waking up with morning hard-ons and partially wet undies from a wet dream. Stud used to be like Unknown. Hell, Stud was Unknown.

Stud, he was waking up with the only thought of making a booty call at ten in the morning. He says, "The morning had barely begun, people at work waiting for their lunch break, and me, I'm flipping through my directory to find someone to have sex with. Waking up to find myself masturbating to a magazine, ala Prince lyrics."

Every action Unknown did was mirrored by Anonymous was mirrored by Stud. Stud used to be a sex addict. That was before he contracted the disease.

Of all the women Stud has slept with, the dancers at the club and the miscellaneous ones he had picked up, it was this doctor, this bleeping doctor who shattered his invincibility and made him as fragile as he was. He was fragile like the front door's mirror. Stud says, "As long as the patron keeps avoiding the situation, the spider web will remain."

Of all the women Stud has slept with, it was the "clean" one of the batch, the respected doctor. Stud, he says, "You would think sleeping with a bunch of strippers would make you the poster boy for the Center of Disease Control, but sometimes you just don't know about a person."

There's a poster with a dog being neutered. The dog's face, it's priceless. The caption reads, "Pain, it's what changes a life."

To the other ghosts in the pipes, Stud says, "Herpes is my way of being neutered. Imagine a poster of me getting my nuts cut off. My facial expression would be just like that dog's."

Stud has been with all the dancers at his club, the veterans at least. Every once in a while a new girl will start out, she'll last a couple weeks and then she's gone. To another club, a topless one, or she upgrades to a full nude one. Recycled strippers, it's what the strip club connoisseurs call them. Stud, he says, "Girls that find themselves working at every club in the area, only to end up at the same one they started. But sometimes, they leave for good."

The patrons, they tell these girls that the money's better. Then she's gone. There is no notice, nothing. Stud says, "And there's no chance to bed her."

Occasionally, one dancer will leave to work for a regular who comes in, at a construction company, answering phones in an office, or selling parts for a 1980 Monte Carlo. Stud, he says, "Sometimes she'll last and then sometimes I'll see her back at Dancers spinning herself around the pole with dollars scattered on the stage below her. All this while Korn is rocking out on the speaker system."

No one knows Stud's profession, except for Lydia, the philosophical one. She says, "Why are you ashamed about owning a strip club? It pays the bills, right?"

"The truth is," Stud says, "I'm not ashamed." He says, "What I'm ashamed about is the reason I bought Dancers was to boost my self-esteem."

Stud slides down in front of his toilet, his knees beginning to hurt from kneeling on the concrete floor. He stretches his legs out and says, "Having girls naked around me, there's a feeling that I can talk to them more loosely than if they were girls I meet at bars. For some reason, clothing makes a world of difference. It would be a similar situation talking to a group of nudists but since I haven't come across any, I'm not so sure."

Stud is what Unknown has been preaching about. An anonymous guy with nothing better to do than to draw attention to himself, whatever that attention may be. Unknown, his goal is to convince people like Stud, like Tex, like Ambiguous, like Nose, etc. etc. to feel good about the crimes they've committed.

Unknown, he's the host to this prisoner party. When the other inmates forget about their crimes,

Unknown jumps into their lives to remind them. Unknown says, "You're all here for a reason, to commit crimes." Unknown says this because he lives it. He says this because he believes it. His answering machine, it's now filled with messages from his godmother asking if he likes macaroni and cheese.

These drain pipe sessions, according to Unknown, they are a means to pour your heart out to one another about anything and everything. He says, "It doesn't matter who is listening or what you say aloud. If it helps you heal inside, then that's all that matters."

Stud says, "Having girls naked around me, I've already seen their goods and something about that makes it easier to drop in complimentary lines that may be deemed as sexual harassment anywhere else."
Lines like, "Do you fuck as good as you look?"

"Normally I don't stare at a woman's breasts but since they're right there."

"I find it hard talking to you. But that's because I have a hard-on."

Like Unknown, Stud is full of them. He says, "Having girls naked around me, it makes it easier to talk to them because I know their situations on why they became dancers. They look at me as the boss, the one who affords them to make a living."

Melody, she's a high school drop out who got kicked out of her parents' house because she got a DUI. She says, "I needed money so I started dancing." She tells this to anyone with a dollar. Her mentality is, "If you don't already feel sorry for me for being a high school dropout, how about if I told you that I got kicked out for driving under the influence?" This usually doubles her income.

One patron, he's been coming around so he can bed Melody, says, "They were mad at you because you got a DUI? Now what?" This patron, he's a good listener, all for the sake of getting laid. Because, according to Unknown, according to Stud, "It's a job. But instead of getting paid, I get laid."

Melody is dancing for money, rubbing her tits in people's faces, namely men old enough to be her father and not once, has she inquired about getting her GED. Men, they're saying when she passes by, "I have pubic hair older than her."

Melody, she says, "My parents kicked me out because I got a DUI."

She says, "My parents hate me because I dance nude."

She says, "My parents don't want to speak to me anymore. They pretend I don't even exist." Now, Melody, she's buying stripper clothes at a store run by a former dancer named Vixen. She says, "Two fucking dresses cost me a hundred fifty dollars." And patrons, they listen to her, all so they can dip their sausage into her fresh gravy.

Unknown, he says, "Daddy issue, it's the number one method of dipping your sausage into fresh gravy."

Stud, he says, "Outside the club, when people, and by people I mean women, ask me what I do for a living, I tell them I'm an investor. Real estate, small businesses, stocks, mutual funds, futures, commodities, stuff like that. One time I invested in, if you can imagine this, a boy's voice."

This boy, he had the voice of Barry White but, like lots of musical dreamers, it went nowhere. Of course, there was no boy; rather it was just a ploy to impress a woman whose favorite artist was, you guessed it, Barry White. Stud, he says, "Tech stocks are my favorite to invest in." Like the mother preaching on television about her sick child, Stud plays with people's emotions to get what he wants. This is how he copes with his insecurity. This is how he copes with his depression.

This spiel, perfected by Unknown, and now practiced by Stud, it takes about a half a minute and then it's, "Can I buy you a drink?" Money is what these women see. Something they don't understand is what they see. Stud says, "Stocks and financing equals money to them. They don't understand it so they don't invest but they know their CEO has stock options and he's rich. Money, ka ching, el dinero, green, take it to the bank, Holy shit I'm rich."

When Stud looks into the mirror, disease is what he sees. He sees a human outline with nothing more than little spots, different colors like a weather map showing extreme conditions. On Stud's chest, there's a tornado approaching. On his legs, there's hail the size of golf balls. On his face, there are humongous sun spots that could be dangerous if too close. Stud, he says, "When I look into the mirror, disease is what I see. On my back, there's a Category 5 hurricane."

Lydia, she says, "Why be embarrassed about what you do? It pays the bills, right?" She's been helping Stud get through his issue and, as far as every prisoner listening knows, has never slept with Stud. Lydia's attempts make little headway but she keeps trying, almost like a therapist getting paid by the hour.

At the club, the girls, they all hit on Stud. Money, is what they see. The owner is what they see. The one who affords them a living is what they see.

Stud, he says, "Me, is what they see."

All the time, every night, is what they see. They don't have time to meet regular men, men who can be found scouring the bars until their cars are the only ones in the parking lot or on side streets. Men out so late the street lights are about to turn off.

While men are at work at the office, the strippers are sleeping like they're vampires in a B-movie. Just one bad move and you're now out late feasting on vampire strippers who take your money. Stud, he says, "But don't change the channel on Lou's TV. He's got seniority. He's the one the vampire strippers are protecting in this morbid, horribly filmed B-movie."

Unknown, through the drains, says, "A B-movie that I'm holding auditions for at this hotel room."

Prisoners laugh, their laughter echoing down the pipes until they exit each inmate's empty bowl.

Stud, he says, "The girls that dance for me, they work until closing time and then go home and sleep until the next day when the sun is at its full potential or Oprah is giving out cars to her audience, only to see the process repeat itself."

Stud's been with so many women he can't keep them all straight. Half of them go forgotten in his memory, along with what he wore the week before or what he had to eat three nights prior. His memory loss, Lydia says, it's common in people like Stud.

"Eventually, I'm going home with them," Stud says. He says, "Actually, we're screwing in the club's VIP area after the last bouncer has punched out. Actually, we're screwing in the club's office, my office, after the waitress has been walked out to her car. Actually, we're screwing up on the bar when there are two cars left parked outside. Screwing on the stage, the pole, it's often cold on your skin. If the police came in with a black light, the club would look like a techno dance club with all the bright stains representing glow sticks."

However, what the girls don't know is, the money isn't that good. Stud, he's able to pay for his own place and his car with ease, but it's not the million dollar enterprise they probably expect.

Lydia, she says, "Tell me about your childhood. What was your mother like?" She says this when she calls him everyday. Stud, in his living room, leaned back against his couch, his socks falling off his feet, he's being blitzed with questions about his childhood. Lydia, she says, "Were you ever physically abused as a child?"

Lydia, this philosophical woman, she likes to get inside Stud's head. She says, "Your actions lead me to believe you're disconnecting yourself from some childhood trauma. It's as if you're using dissociation to reduce a strain."

Stud's finances, they are not like the girls imagine. There is no sports car or some fancy house in the country. There are no other businesses. There is no living it up like Hugh Hefner, living in some mansion where women walk around topless. There are no tennis courts, game houses or Grotto. There's no Drew Carey or other celebrities walking around with martinis and wide smiles. There are no marble floors, no nice spas, no saunas, and no mirrors above the bed. And there is no spare bedroom with walk-in closets and personal bathrooms with full length mirrors.

Stud says, "How about an Olympic sized swimming pool? Yeah right."

He says, "How about a personal chef? Not even close."

He says, "How about a limo to drive us around? Give me a break." Stud, he stands from his position, leans down, places his hands on his hips and yells into the drains. "There is none of that. What I do have is credit card debt and some mildew in the bathtub. There's a spider that spins a web every day in the corner of the kitchen. There are crumbs living in the cracks on the counter top. And then there's rent for the building, payment for the electricity, the bouncers, waitresses, bartenders, and deejays."

Lydia, playing doctor, she says, "How long were you abused? How long have you been traumatized?" She says, into the phone, her voice soothing to the ear, "Have you ever had the chance to deal with your problems? Not dealing with your problems eliminates the ability to deal with issues in adulthood."

Stud, continuing his story like he's giving a speech to a tuned in audience, says, "I've got the licensing, the building maintenance, taxes, and fees I had no idea even existed. Those ones hurt because they come out of nowhere. But I manage."

Pain is what changes a life. Stud, is what these women see. Unknown is what they see. Unknown, he comes in three times a week, to say hi, to get drunk, and to flirt with the girls.

Madison, she's a once married, the biggest mistake of her life, mother of four. She has twins and then a daughter and then a son. In that order. Her cheap department store glasses slide down her nose when she twirls around the pole. Her long, greasy hair falls down the sides of her head and brushes against her boobs when she spins in her high heels. She talks to you with her cute little voice, the entire time while dollars protrude from her G-string. She wants nothing to do with Unknown but Unknown unloads pick up lines on her because he sees the children and uses them to his advantage.

Unknown, he says, "She has to be a slut. Three kids?"

Stud says, "Four. She has four."

"Four kids?" Unknown hits on Ariel, the Iranian beauty who speaks choppy English and is in the country on a school visa. She's studying communications and one of the lessons Unknown tries teaching her is, "Call me." She laughs but she believes Unknown is joking. She says, "You funny." She says, "You cute." And then she offers to go back to the private dance area. Ariel, her brown skin and long, black hair, dark features make for a knockout. Regulars, they're saying, "That one doesn't even have pubic hair."

Lydia says to Stud, "In your adulthood you may cope differently with each traumatic event. I'm surprised you're not seeing this."

The regulars at Dancers, they eye Ariel when she leaves the stage. The men, they leave dollars on the foot of the stage, scattered like a deck of cards and whoever has the best hand wins a trip to the private dance area. Ariel walks around, as if she's playing a game of Duck, Duck, Private Dance. The men, they're sitting up straight to get the best exposure, hoping that Ariel taps them on the shoulder and says, "Private Dance."

There's a picture with dogs playing poker, and the caption beneath it reads, "Life is like a poker hand, either bluff your way through or fold."

Unknown, he doesn't cause trouble so Stud lets him stay. Stud says, "I let him stay because we're close. Pete, though, causes trouble so I don't let him stay."

"Be on the lookout for a man wearing sunglasses impersonating a blind man." This is the notice that circulates every month. The notice, spreading the word about some pervert, goes in and out of email accounts until the word gets out. It goes in and out of mailboxes until the impersonator is identified. Random phone messages say to be on the lookout for a blind man.

Lydia says, "Your sex addiction began in childhood and is continuing in adulthood. That's why you own a strip club. You're staying in that atmosphere longer than any person should." Lydia highlights a page, flips it and begins reading more to Stud. She says, "You hang out with Unknown, someone who has slept with 150 women. Does that seem normal to you?"

Stud, he says, "A blind man in a strip club, well, he has to feel his way through."

Lydia tells Stud that his best friends are a con man and a group of girls who have been kicked out of their house for petty crime. She says, "Oh, and Lou. But he's only nice to you because you let him watch music stations."

Pete, unfortunately, is not blind. He's not even close. He doesn't wear glasses or contacts. In fact, Pete has perfect vision. He plays the part in a strip club, wearing thick black sunglasses, so the girls feel sorry for him. The dancers, they grab his hands and place them on their boobs. Stud, he says, "It's a sympathy pat down."

Lydia, she says, "Where is your family? Is your mother still alive?" She puts down a book and picks up another one, with various cases of people acting like Stud. "I just read a story about a person like you. He was both abused and neglected as a child. Those two things could be detrimental to you as an adult."

Pete, he has a smile from ear to ear and his dark sunglasses are reflecting sets of boobs outwardly. His glasses, they can usually be seen on an elderly woman behind the wheel of a Cadillac.

Pete, he says, "I didn't do anything." He says this after he's successfully groped four sets of breasts. Pete says, "They put my hands up there. You can't fault me for that." Then he says, as security guards make their way to him, "What? You're kicking me out?"

Stud, he says, "Good riddance."

And Lydia, flipping through pages and pages of self-help books, highlighting paragraphs along the way, says, "You said your herpes make you depressed? Your depression and anxiety come from your low self-esteem." She says, "And Unknown? How much time does he waste saving nude photos on his computer and masturbating when he could be working a real job?"

Stud says, "Unknown used to be in love with this woman, Beverly. This was years ago. She broke his heart and his insecurity won't allow him to commit to anyone. Instead, he sleeps with as many women as possible to somehow get back at her for cheating on him. I won't let that happen to me."

Lydia, she says, "Is that true about Unknown? His actions tell me something entirely different." She says, "You really need to start looking at everything you do and see how it affects the people around you. Once you've done that, start looking at how your actions affect you, your self-esteem, your mood, your health."

Unknown doesn't want Stud to pull the plug on his highly ambitious efforts of hitting on the girls. Stud says, "As long as you're not touching them in the building, what they do in their off time is not my business."

Tara is a first year college drop out. She calls it taking a break. Tara, she's a five foot tall, 90 pound wonder. All natural and she likes women. This is what she tells Unknown at least. She says, "I'm going to have sex later. With my girlfriend."

"Let's make it a threesome." Unknown says. He says, "I'll bring beer." Unknown, he's telling her that he has thousands of dollars in accounts all over the world. "Seriously, I should take you to the Bahamas with me."

Tara tells Unknown to go get some pot. She says, "Maybe we'll talk later." Then Unknown is gone, in search for weed and when he returns, an hour later, Tara has cashed out early for the night, paying the $50 dollars "exit early rule" to the house to avoid seeing Unknown.

Unknown says to Stud, "Where'd she go?"

Stud says, "She was sick. She left." Stud has slept with Tara many times. According to Stud, she's good in bed, very tight. Very sensual, makes for a great dancer.

Lydia asks Stud, "Have any of the girls accused you of giving them herpes?"

Stud, he says, "Since I've been infected, I'm not at the club as much. My manager, she works the bar and does the books. Every now and then she calls and asks if something is wrong.

"Just been busy."

She thinks the place is going to shut down. On the news, the city is trying to clamp down on adult oriented businesses in the area. Only five licenses are available and they want it dropped to four. Stud says, "It pretty much means one strip club has to shut down."

Stud, he says, "No one wants to give so my staff thinks it might be my club because it has the least amount of seniority in the city. There's me with seven years. There's Gents with twelve years. There's Kitty Kat Klub with sixteen years. And then there's the old timers, Al's and Sensations."

The news story, it reports that the city wants to license all the girls and have them all required to get background checks, like they're criminals or something. Times like this are when the strip clubs unite and work together as one. At a city council meeting, all the girls who are married and have families step forward and give statements, saying that it isn't right to treat them like bad people.

Alexa, she says, "I am a wife and a mother of three. I live a normal life but I happen to be a dancer. I don't do drugs and just because I take me clothes off for a living, it doesn't mean that I'm a drug addict or a criminal."

Then she sits down, only to see this process repeated. Ruby, she says, "I'm putting myself through school and I'm going to be a nurse."

Then there is Ginger. She says, "Just because you work in an office or have a nine to five job, it doesn't mean that you're not a drug addict." She says, "Why don't you license them too?"

The city's stance behind this one isn't as strong as the license issue so having only four licenses is the main business. Stud, he says, "Thank goodness for this. I'm running out of married dancers. If it comes up again, all my single dancers will have to give a married woman statement."

Stud, he says to Lydia, in between preaching and flipping pages, "Since I've been infected, I haven't slept with any of the girls. The girls all think that I have a girlfriend now, someone who is hindering my coming in."

Lydia says, "I'm proud of you. You seem to care about these girls more than you think. You're like a father figure to them." She says, "Is your father still around? And if so, have you spoken to your father in a while?"

Unknown, without Stud around, hits on all of them, more than once and sometimes, twice in the same night. Stud says through the pipes, his voice now getting tired and beginning to sound like a ghost, "It's like a little family inside Dancers, but outside, in my own private life, it's unscrewing light bulbs only to replace them again."

Pain is what changes a life.

Lydia, though, she's proud of Stud. Lydia says, "I think if you use that care on yourself like you do for your girls, your life will be more fruitful."

One ghost, through the pipes, says, "Speaking of fruitful, my come is full of fruit. Do you think Lydia wants it?" And then there's a flush.

19.

Pete will do anything. That's what they say about him. He'll do anything to get away with something. The blind guy routine at a strip club, that's just one of the things.

He says, "Sometimes, I'll just be sitting there and shit will come flying out of my mouth." Pete, he lies to women, telling them that he's a voice over artist who does nothing but sit in an edit bay all day. He says, "Foreign pornos that come through the country, I sit in a booth with headphones on saying things like, 'ooh,' 'yes,' 'magnifico.'"

Pete, he says this stuff to anyone listening. He says, "Right there, right there, right there," as he pretends to drops his pants to his ankles and beat himself like he's in a contest. His pants are collecting dust on the bottom of his legs. His knees are bony and hairless and Pete, he's going to town on his penis. "Yeah, right there baby."

He says, "I feel sorry for the guy who cleans those bays." People, women mainly, they say, "That's not a job, is it?" Pete, he says, "When I was in college, this guy whose dad is in the Adult Filmmakers Union..." Pete, he feigns ignorance, as if everyone should know what the Adult Filmmakers Union is. "He got me a job unpacking videos..." Pete shrugs his shoulder, he gestures this is my life. "His dad says, the videos come off the truck, you unpack them, scan them, and put them back on the belt."

Titles like Open For Business, A Hole In One, and Good Vibrations, they're just a few. He says, "I've seen ones like Exchange Students, Sex Visa, and Love Me Long Time."

After a few months, Pete says, "I'm now in the union and I can't believe my life has come to this. I'm in college for Business Administration and now I'm administering my business." He winks, because this is funny to him. "Now I do it full-time. Sitting there in the bay, alone, watching pornography that I can't understand. Only in America." He shakes his head, wondering how he got into this situation.

Lydia says, about people like Pete, about people like Stud, and about people like Unknown, "You're losing your ability to understand what is real and what is not. There is a term for people that show shortages in tests of cognizant control." She says, turning page after page of self-help books and medical guides, "It's an illness, usually starting from your childhood. What happened in your childhood that you don't want to talk about?""

At Dancers, Pete's telling the girls that he has a bizarre, rare condition that he can't see too much nudity at one time. He says, to Angel, a curly haired woman with sympathy to men with dollar bills, "It sucks. I'd like to sit at the stage but you have to show my one boob at a time." Pete, he says, "And tell the girls that go on after you too."

Angel, naive to the potential dollars, the bills that pay her rent and cell phone, she says, "What happens if you see too much nudity?" She says, showing one boob at a time as if it's a perverted game of peek-a-boob.

Stud, he says into the pipes, "Peek-a-boob, I'm full of them."

Pete says that he'll wet himself and that it would be a good idea if he didn't. He says, "I could start wearing brown corduroy pants here, because if I wet myself, no one will be able to tell." He says this to Angel, to any girl that will buy it. This, to Pete, is funny.

Pete's actions, they have no care for the reactions of others on the receiving end. So long as he gets what he needs, he's fine. Unknown, he says that society coddles people and that each of them is responsible for rules that protect the coddled. He says this because his mother abused him. He says this because his godmother coddled him. He blames society for this happening. Unknown, he does these things when he's feeling wanted.

Angel, she's nodding her head in agreement, all for a dollar or two, and possibly a half-assed private dance where she strips very slowly to cater to Pete. She says, "Why don't you get on meds?"

Meds, they're something Pete says he will get on once his insurance kicks in. Again, it's a union issue, something about not paying union dues; this is fuzzy but funny nonetheless.

Lydia, she says, "Stud, I think you should get on medication as well. I've heard enough from you to get a handle of what you're dealing with. Your herpes, it's a means to avoid the bigger picture."

Angel, she feels sorry for Pete and every time she sees him, standing off to the side of the stage, she says, "Have you gotten on meds yet?"

She says, "How many videos have you watched this week?"

She says, "Is the edit bay just filled with urine from seeing too much nudity?"

And Pete, he's scrambling to say something, anything. "The meds are worth it," he says, "thanks for asking." And then Pete takes a trip to the private dance area where Angel lets loose and throws his face into her chest like he's looking out a periscope.

For full effect, Pete closes his eyes and pushes, like he's giving birth. He winces in pain from trying to excrete anything from his body. While Angel's boobs are in his face, Pete pushes harder until a few tiny droplets of urine come out. He says, "Oh shit, I just peed a little."

He says this so Angel feels sorry for him. She says, stopping instantly and covering up her breasts with her bikini top that is pulled down to her ribcage, "Oh my God! I'm sorry. Is there anything I can do?"

And Pete, slightly wet from piss and his body cramped from pushing, says, "Could you help me get home? My meds are there."

She smiles, nods and says, "Give me a couple minutes. I'll pay to leave early."

As Pete makes his way around the stage, Stud motions to the bouncer to toss him. Pete watches the men surround him. He does this while Angel disappears into the dressing room to gather her belongings. The bouncers grab each arm and push him toward the exit.

The girls, they see Pete getting tossed, and say to each other and to random customers they're near, "Be careful. He's on medication."

Pete, he says, walking swift with the bouncer's hands pushing behind him, "My doctor says I need these."

Pete says, "My eyes are dilated."

Pete says, "I have a note."

And as he passes Stud, Stud says, "Good riddance."

Angel, in the dressing room, realizes she's been duped. "I thought he needed help," she says. "I thought I could help him."

The voices in the drainpipes, shooting out of the toilet bowls, they're talking about their lives when they get out. "When I get outta here," a voice says, "I'm going to change my life."

Another voice, it says, "Me too."

"I'm serious," the first ghost says, "no more bullshit for me."

"Thanks for the stories," one voice says. And then a flush.

Lydia says, "You should use your story about Pete as an example. Once you get on medication, you can strive to fix yourself too."

These stories, the facts and the fictions often get misconstrued. Unknown, he is lying on his bed about to fall asleep. He's listening to the stories, telling his own, in some way he's united the guys. He yells out loud, so that all the inmates can hear his voice traveling through the drainpipes, "When you finally leave this dump, just remember that you're anonymous." He says, "No one will know what you're about. That's where you have the upper hand, knowing something that they don't. Don't ever give that up."

The stories, they get misconstrued as the facts aren't really facts and the fictions aren't really fictions. Sometimes, the people telling the stories aren't who they appear to be. Sometimes, the voices sound the same and you never really know where they're coming from. And sometimes, the same person just keeps telling the same story, over and over until he's sick in the head.

Unknown says, "When you finally get out of here, your actions will determine if you return." His voice, it's the only one that's ever remembered. It's the one that sticks in your mind anytime you reflect on the drainpipe sessions.

Unknown, Stud, Tex, Ambiguous, Anonymous, Pete, Nose, and so on and so on, his mother abused him both physically and sexually. His mother, she forced him to role play on Thursdays. She told him she'd bring him home an ice cream cone. His godmother, she coddled him too much. So much so he couldn't deal with life. So much so he began a life of cons and sex addiction. The combination of child raising, it was too much for him to handle.

His mother, now back in the real world, and living a quiet life back home in Nebraska, she's asking why her son has severe memory loss, mood swings and different personalities. She asks this to his doctor, his nurses, anyone that can give answers. She asks about the distortion of subjective time, the flashbacks of abuse, and identity confusion.

The voice in the pipes, the voice in his head, it says, "You matter in society. People will never forget you."

His mother, she spoon fed him cold medicine to look sick, and now she's asking why her son is so screwed up. Her son's adopted mother, she won't answer calls because she hasn't forgiven yet.

"She won't even talk to me," she says. "I let her raise my child."

The symptoms, they cross identities whenever he switches. Sometimes he doesn't even know he's doing it. There are multiple personalities living inside him, sometimes all at the same time, coming out to talk, to tell stories, to cope with life.

This illness, called Dissociative Identity Disorder, it's what causes the many attitudes and mannerisms. The voices, they're often psychotic and self-destructive, suicidal and unexplainable. Each day can be a challenge. Each day, he can go from totally low to severely impaired and from normal to ridiculously high. All like a flip of the switch. All at once.

Lydia, she says, "The researcher Putnam describes these personalities as 'highly discrete states of consciousness organized around a prevailing affect, sense of self (including body image), with a limited repertoire of behaviors and a set of state dependent memories.'" She says, "This could explain why he's basically the same person yet experiences different emotions amongst each personality."

The traits, they are all around one host that controls the traumatic background. Lydia says, "It's almost as if the one called Unknown wrote a movie script and has the alternates playing along. Unknown is the narrator in this multi-faceted tale."

The suggested treatment for this illness is psychotherapy. Lydia, she says, "We need to get the multiple identities integrated into one, cohesive personality. Keep in mind, people who suffer from DID honestly believe they have different people living inside them, taking over their bodies when they come out."

About 1% of the population may suffer from Dissociative Identity Disorder. And right now, you're doing the math to see how many people that actually is. There are more than 7,000,000,000 (billion) people in the world. That's something like 70 million people possibly walking around with multiple personalities. Your neighbor, your boss, your spouse, each could potentially be a walking movie, worrying about the newest trends and latest fashions so that one or two or all personalities feel important. Lydia, she says, "If anything, we need each personality to play nice to each other."

Specialists, on television, peddling their books or new programs, they're saying, "This is an ongoing problem for sure. Buy my book and you'll know the keys to managing this illness. After all, an A-lister whole heartedly approves of my product."

This prison, it's not really a prison. Well, not the kind you'd think of. This mental institution, it's a means to keep Unknown safe, safe from society, his mother, and people that coddle him. And people that abuse him. The world, it needs people like Unknown.

If anything, to make him feel important.

If anything, to make him feel relevant.

"The conning, the stalking, the stalking, the conning, the sexual addiction, they're all anonymous to me." He says, "I don't even know who I am anymore. The facts and fictions, they make me unknown to myself. What's true? What's not? My childhood? My adulthood? My scams? My addiction? I am anonymous."

Unknown, he talks to himself each day, telling himself stories, exchanging dialog, and laughing to himself. Sometimes he cries, sometimes he's angry, and sometimes his pants are down to his ankles and his penis is erect. Sometimes the stories are so true he gets mad at himself for being fooled.

His mother, she's writing to her congressman because people are taking her son away from her. She says, "I'm a good mother. Why are they doing this?" She says this on television, with tears in her eyes, and a congressman in her corner. There is a picture of her son on an easel so everyone can see his smiling face.

Her story, it's informing people, viewers, victims that her son was taken away from her for no real reason. She says, "My son needs his mother. His illness can only be treated with motherly love. I have set up a foundation for you to donate. Every little bit helps."

Some viewers, they're writing to this woman, sympathizing with her because they have children of their own. They're shaking their heads in disgust, hoping that a reunion is in the works. Other viewers, they're changing the channels saying, "What else is on television?"

Lydia, she monitors his improvement through a one way see through window, recording his progress and suggesting anecdotes to help him heal. A microphone and speaker are set up so she can talk to him out of harm's way.

"We're going to start you on psychotherapy," Lydia says. She says, "It can be a very long process, often times arduous and tiring. This may trigger every bad memory you've ever had in your life." The therapy, it can take several years and there is no guarantee that a person with DID will ever be healed.

Lydia, flipping through pages and pages of medical journals and self-help books, she highlights various illnesses that have similar symptoms.

Lydia, playing doctor, says into a handheld recorder, "As much as we'd like to think this is DID, I don't think this is the right diagnosis. DID can often times be misdiagnosed for other illnesses. Have we considered Narcissistic Personality Disorder? Let's keep him here for more observation."

His mother, she's saying, "Please help me get my son back. Don't let these people do the same to you what they've done to me." She sniffles, and then looks at her son's picture to add to the effect. "Have a heart, donate money now. And contact your congressman today about how you can help spread the word."

And specialists, they're saying, "It's an ongoing problem for sure."

Jason Tanamor

CPSIA information can be obtained at www.ICGtesting.com
Printed in the USA
LVOW06s1112090314

376609LV00003B/522/P